# AFTERNOON DELIGHT

As if on cue, Matthew appeared before Sarah. He smiled and held out a gloved hand.

"Come, Sarah. We will show them how it should be done. Let me help you." He led her to a bench and took her skates from her. Removing his gloves, he knelt before her to fit the blades to her boots. "We have been here before, have we not?" He laughed up at her. "Only this time your ankle is in perfect order." He surreptitiously caressed her leg.

"Matthew!" The laughter in her voice belied the admonishment as she pushed his hand away and readjusted the hem of her cloak. He grinned, put his gloves back on, and led her onto the ice.

They skated smoothly and sedately together for a round or two. Then, gaining momentum and enthusiasm, they twirled and danced on the ice, their movements becoming faster and more intricate. Having, indeed, shown the others, they graciously acknowledged a round of applause and continued.

Unable to suppress a gurgle of laughter, Sarah was happily startled to see her exhilaration mirrored in Matthew's eyes. And something else—naked hunger that sent a surge of warmth swirling through her. . . .

# BOOK YOUR PLACE ON OUR WEBSITE AND MAKE THE READING CONNECTION!

We've created a customized website just for our very special readers, where you can get the inside scoop on everything that's going on with Zebra, Pinnacle and Kensington books.

When you come online, you'll have the exciting opportunity to:

- View covers of upcoming books
- Read sample chapters
- Learn about our future publishing schedule (listed by publication month *and author*)
- Find out when your favorite authors will be visiting a city near you
- Search for and order backlist books from our online catalog
- Check out author bios and background information
- Send e-mail to your favorite authors
- Meet the Kensington staff online
- Join us in weekly chats with authors, readers and other guests
- Get writing guidelines
- AND MUCH MORE!

**Visit our website at
http://www.zebrabooks.com**

# WILLED
# TO WED

## *Wilma Counts*

Zebra Books
Kensington Publishing Corp.
http://www.zebrabooks.com

ZEBRA BOOKS are published by

Kensington Publishing Corp.
850 Third Avenue
New York, NY 10022

First Printing: September, 1999
10 9 8 7 6 5 4 3 2 1

Printed in the United States of America

*For Nisha and Grant,*
*who know the meaning of love—*
*and friendship*

# One

"What in blazes are you doing here so early?" Matthew Carey Cameron, major in His Majesty's forces, veteran of the Peninsular campaign, and newly elevated peer of the realm, glared through sleep-befuddled eyes at the visitor who casually invaded his bedchamber.

Adrian Whitson, Marquis of Trenville, was impeccably attired in a dark blue coat sporting the unmistakable elegance of Weston. Matthew closed his eyes against the gleaming Hessian boots and snowy cravat—and against the brilliant display of white teeth in his best friend's broad grin.

"Too early," Matthew groaned, but he swung his legs out of bed and reached for the large mug of strong coffee offered by his batman, Coop.

"Early? It is past noon already! And you asked me to stop by. I must say, if your appearance at the moment is an indication of what His Majesty's troops are come to, I fear for England's safety should Napoleon's present misfortunes take a turn for the better."

Matthew grunted. "If that happens, I trust we can count on you soldiers of peace in the foreign office to sweet-talk him into giving up forthwith!" He waved his hand toward the desk. "Those are the papers I had from the solicitor. Do look them over, Adrian. Find me a way out of this infernal situation. As a lawyer and a diplomat, surely you can come up with something. Imagine me—leg-shackled at my tender age."

Adrian's disdainful "Hah!" reminded the new earl that he and his friend were of an age, both thirty-one. The marquis, married at twenty-three, had lost his wife in child-birth two years later.

As Matthew shaved, dressed, and brought himself more firmly into the world of human beings with minimal help from Coop, Adrian perused the document and drank the coffee Coop brought him.

"Hmmm. Well-l-l-l . . ." Adrian drew the word out dubiously. "This is not my general area of law, but it appears rather tight to me. Your uncle and the lady's grandfather seem to have had some pretty astute minds at work on this."

"That is not what I want to hear."

"Of course, they assumed that the Seventh Earl would be your cousin Robert. But I doubt an unwritten assumption would carry much weight if it actually went to court." Adrian's brown eyes twinkled. "Maybe you should just marry the lady."

"Easy for you to say. You are not the one looking into the barrel of the matrimonial gun. She must be a real antidote."

"What makes you think so?"

"She must be lacking in appearance, character, or fortune—why else would anyone go to such lengths to get her married?" Matthew ran his hand through a shock of light brown hair. "Why me?" he wailed in mock despair. "Here I am, home from the wars just this week—I should be able to stroll into a ballroom and have my pick of pretty lasses, and what happens? Those bloody wills! I'd rather be back on the battlefield."

Now prepared to face the day, he dismissed Coop.

"You were managing that 'home from the wars' role pretty well last night at the Billington rout. Marriage need not inhibit your style too awfully, old chap."

"Just as it did not inhibit you, eh?" Matthew's tone was heavy with friendly sarcasm.

"Different story. But you were drawing them like flies to honey last night."

"I had forgotten what empty-headed foolishness one spouts in polite society. All those pretty flowers of the *ton*—schoolroom misses fishing for compliments on their hair ribbons or some such. Females in the demimonde are more honest!"

"Speaking of female honesty—or lack of it—you might be interested to know that Annalisa Poindexter is on the prowl again. Her elderly husband prefers the country, but the beautiful Annalisa has not lost her taste for town. She asked about you."

Matthew froze as he reached for his hat. Only Adrian would dare bring up her name, and so lightheartedly at that. Only Adrian understood what the lovely Annalisa—she of the silvery blond hair and emerald eyes—had meant to him. Even now, nearly ten years later, the pain haunted him.

"Hmph." Matthew wished he could ignore the topic. "I saw her when I was back four or five years ago. She seemed satisfied with the position and purse her marriage brought."

"She should have been. It was a sizable purse."

"I never understood . . ."

"What? How she could forsake your sterling self for all that delicious money?"

"Well, that, too. But why she kept me dangling after her. Two days—two days!—before her wedding she and I were still planning to elope."

"Perhaps she could not face the prospect of scandal. Annalisa does enjoy her place on the social ladder."

"She used me to bring Poindexter up to scratch. But there was no need to keep me on a leash once he had offered." Matthew fought to keep his voice neutral. Good God! Could she still tie him in knots?

"Annalisa thrives on male attention. She needs to feel every man in her sphere wants her. Once she makes a conquest, she moves on. Ironically, her marriage has allowed a certain amount of freedom in that regard."

"In the end, she certainly fared better with Poindexter

than she would have, had she accepted the pathetic offer of a besotted young soldier."

"Perhaps the young soldier fared better, too," Adrian said quietly. Matthew did not respond. Then Adrian asked, "Do you recall a cousin of hers named Hamilton Ridgeley?"

"Very well. Used to play too deep for my pockets. Likable chap, though."

"He still loves a game. He also squires the lovely Annalisa when she seems between . . . uh . . . liaisons."

Matthew chuckled derisively. "So that's the polite term these days, eh? . . . Even as children she and Ridgeley were close. She could always persuade him to do whatever she wanted." He pointed at the papers still in Adrian's hand to redirect the discussion. "Well?"

Adrian looked thoughtful for a moment. "You know, I think I may know your intended bride. Seaverton took his position in the House of Lords seriously. Good friend of Castlereagh and our office. The granddaughter used to act as his hostess. Not such an antidote at all, Matt, old man. Not at all. I remember dark hair and violet eyes, I think. Or were the eyes blue? Maybe gray. Intelligent, though, and well-read."

"Wonderful! Just what I need—some bluestocking to preach sermons at me on a regular basis. And do stop referring to her as my intended! I tell you, there must be some way out of this broil."

It occurred to him that this outburst directly contradicted what he had objected to in "schoolroom misses." He was glad Trenville chose to ignore it as the two set out for White's.

A few days later, the new Lord Markholme had consulted several notable men of law in London as well as an army of creditors holding notes against his new properties. Their collective judgment was that if he intended to accept the inheritance, he needed to find some way to ensure its fiscal survival.

To obtain a complete view of the situation, he set off
for Derbyshire to inspect the main property which he had
last seen as a youthful visitor. He invited his friend Adrian
Whitson and Richard Hendley, a young lieutenant who
served in his regiment, to accompany him.

He would also call upon the lady in question. He expected little to come of such a meeting. Trust a woman
again? Not bloody likely!

And certainly not *this* woman. After all, her mother destroyed the life of Matthew's favorite uncle, his father's
oldest brother. A very young Matthew, having lost his father, had been devastated when his fun-loving adventurous
idol slowly destroyed himself in oceans of alcohol and gaming debts, finally taking his own life. And all because some
mindless chit had thrown him over for a sea captain with
interests in the West Indies.

Later, Matthew himself had not fared much better. On
the threshold of maturity, he, too, encountered a woman
who freely gave sweet kisses and promised undying love—
even as she negotiated for title and wealth elsewhere. Now
he was to welcome some conniving chit to his bed? Not
bloody likely! he repeated to himself.


In Derbyshire, the supposed "antidote" had wrestled
for weeks with the provisions of wills written by her grandfather and his friend on the neighboring estate. Miss Sarah
Matthilde Longbourne knew the details early on, but a
recent visit from the solicitor brought the situation home
to her as her family now fully absorbed the implications.

"Oh, Sarah! It simply cannot be. *Grandpapa* is forcing
you to marry some stranger?" Miss Emily Longbourne
vented shock and outrage in the unrestrained manner of
one having only eighteen years.

"He still controls—even from the grave," said Charles,
brother to the two Longbourne sisters.

Sarah willed herself to sit stoically, her hands clasped
tightly in the folds of her dress. The late September sun

slanted through the library windows, its dancing beams a dramatic contrast to the mood in the room.

"Grandpapa and the Sixth Earl of Markholme wanted to combine their properties. Marriage between the eldest Longbourne daughter and the Seventh Earl was their solution." Sarah did not want Charles and Emily to suspect her own apprehension and anger.

"But that should have been Robert," Charles declared.

"Yes." Sarah remembered fondly the man who had almost become her fiancé. "Grandpapa and the Sixth Earl were sanctioning marriage between Robert and me, but neither will specified names and neither was ever changed."

"Well, it's just not right!" Emily's vehemence was the antithesis of Sarah's calm. "Grandpapa was downright mean not to change his will when Robert was killed."

"I doubt it even occurred to him," Sarah said.

"What do you think of this coil, Aunt Bess?" Emily addressed the fourth person in the room. The widowed Mrs. Carstairs had joined her father's household years before as a surrogate mother to her orphaned nieces and nephew.

"Papa knew what he wanted," Aunt Bess said. "Unfortunately, he tied up the entire estate on this one condition."

Charles snorted. "He was stubborn and strong-willed, you mean."

"He was disappointed neither your mother nor I was the heir he wanted," Aunt Bess replied gently. "Without a son of his own, he could not keep the Seaverton title and entailed properties in the immediate family, but he did control this estate. The will was his way of ensuring his wishes would prevail."

After a pause, Sarah said, "Please. Do not refine upon this too much. It comes as a shock to you, but I knew about the wills—though circumstances were different then."

Emily gestured impatiently. "You cannot just accept this high-handedness, Sarah!"

"You are right, Emily. There is a choice. However, whatever is done will affect not only the four of us, but a good many others as well."

"Who?" Emily demanded.

"Servants. Tenants. People like Lofton, Mrs. Blodgett, the Johnsons. Rosemont is not just a pile of old stones, you know."

"Well, it is not an altar requiring a sacrificial lamb, either," her sister retorted.

Sarah looked at her, startled. Then she laughed. "Oh, dear. Did I sound so very noble? I meant only that what happens to Rosemont concerns many people besides ourselves. And, of course, the situation also involves the new Lord Markholme."

Emily sniffed scornfully. "Who has yet to see it as necessary even to present himself!"

"He has been on the Peninsula," Aunt Bess explained.

"Well, he should be here in Derbyshire," Emily said without regard for reason or calm.

Charles had been quiet during this exchange. "Perhaps if we pool our resources, we could take a cottage somewhere. Surely, we could manage. I might tutor some local boys."

"And give up your idea of a commission?" Emily turned to him aghast. "Besides, you were never such a grand scholar as to think of becoming a tutor. Better you should become a drawing master with your heavy hand on the crayon, or I a dressmaker, renowned seamstress as I am."

"Well, what idea do *you* offer?"

"I think Sarah or I should find a husband with a sizable fortune, preferably a handsome man with an amiable disposition who would fall madly in love with one of us."

"Men with sizable fortunes are not looking to marry penniless chits—even pretty little blondes like you," her brother scoffed. "If that is the plan, Sarah might as well tie herself to Markholme after all."

# Two

Sarah immersed herself in the distracting duties of estate, household, and parish as she pondered the "what ifs" of the future. Others would suffer if she chose wrongly.

She also brooded over the particular question of marriage. Her role as hostess for her grandfather and his political friends had proved more interesting to Sarah than balls and soirees meant to facilitate one's search for a husband. She had long since come to terms with being "on the shelf" when she and Robert Cameron had reached an understanding.

Neither worried that their relationship lacked the passion and intensity of a romance from the Minerva Press. With a marked degree of warm affection, they would "rub on well together." However, before a formal announcement could be made, the gentle, caring Robert was dead, drowned in a boating accident. His optimistic promises—they would marry and, of course, live happily ever after—had turned to ashes.

Robert's death left a void in her life. She had lost a dear friend. She did not feel the loss as a lover, but she refused to dwell on that idea. Marriage was no longer an attractive option—and marriage to a stranger was decidedly unattractive.

Now, it was being thrust upon her.

Sarah had loved her grandfather and understood his benevolent despotism. He adamantly refused to purchase a commission for his grandson whom he considered "too young to go haring off to battle." But he had readily defied society's conventions to allow his granddaughter to share the estate management. His dictatorial power in life had allowed him to control, but in death, it robbed his family of authority over their own destinies.

Since her grandfather was unavailable, Sarah aimed her anger and frustration at the man who now controlled the situation, a shadowy figure off fighting in Spain. Meanwhile, the family looked to her to decide their shared future. And she—who had long been the one in charge—felt trapped in an indecisive state of limbo. And she hated it.

Several days after that meeting in the library, she heaved an exasperated sigh and said to herself, "Oh, well. All right. I will at least consider this marriage." There! *She* had made the decision. So why did she still feel trapped?

From her agent, Mr. Howard, she learned the servants at Markholme Hall expected the new earl and two guests. So, Markholme was finally coming to inspect his lands. Did he also want to look over the prospective bride his uncle had foisted upon him? What kind of man would accept such dictates?

That evening after Lofton had withdrawn from serving tea in the drawing room, Sarah made her announcement.

"The three of you will be interested to know that if Lord Markholme proves agreeable and tolerable, I am prepared to accept the terms of Grandpapa's will."

"Yours is the life that will be most profoundly changed, if you do this, Sarah," Charles said. "For me, you need not make such a sacrifice. I daresay I shall continue to live if I do not become an army officer."

"Nor for me," Emily cried. "Girls marry all the time without a season in London. I own I should like the parties and balls prodigiously, but not if my gaiety means Sarah's misery!"

Genuinely moved by her usually carefree, teasing siblings' concern, Sarah smiled. "I have no intention of becoming a *sacrifice.* I did say *if* Lord Markholme is agreeable and tolerable. . . . We simply do not know yet, do we? So—please—no more about 'Sarah's misery.' "

"I wish I could do more," Charles said. "If only our parents had left us better provided for."

"But they did not. We must face the facts of the matter, however unattractive they may be."

Within hours of his arrival at Markholme Hall, Cameron's presence was known throughout the district and was the instance of considerable nervous apprehension at the adjoining estate.

Sarah arose early the next morning. She had spent a fitful night, beset by doubts and worries, in contrast to the calm self-possession she had shown her family. To prolong the silence and solitude of the night, she decided not to disturb the stable hands for a mount.

Thus it was that, dressed in an old woolen gown of faded blue, a nondescript shawl of darker blue, and wearing serviceable half-boots, she set out on foot for the cottage of her chief tenant farmer a mile and a half away. She carried a basket of herbal teas and medicines, as well as some sweetmeats for the grandmother of the house who suffered a severe case of old age.

Autumn was Sarah's favorite time of the year. She loved the cold, clear tanginess of frosty air, the crunch of leaves underfoot, the variety of earthy colors, and the occasional smell of morning fires. Walking hurriedly to keep warm, she nevertheless relished the chill. Her cheeks tingled and her breath clouded in front of her, making her feel especially alive. As the sun would wash away the chill, the morning chased away the shadows of her night. Disregarding the dampness that soaked her feet and left the hem of her gown wet and soiled, she cut across a pasture, across the country lane leading to the village, and through a copse of maples and birches to the Johnson place.

Later, she retraced her path through the copse, her basket now containing a round of fresh butter and a jar of honey for the Rosemont kitchen. Deep in thought as she started to cross the lane, her mind did not register the sound of pounding hooves. Suddenly, a huge horse appeared directly in front of her. She threw up her hands in a gesture of self-protection, dropping her basket. The startled horse reared suddenly. Flailing hooves forced her to jump backward. Wrenching her ankle viciously, she fell with a scream into the roadside ditch.

She lay there, momentarily stunned, but aware that the rider had not lost his seat and even managed to control his spirited mount. He leapt from the saddle and was at her side instantly.

"My God! Where did you come from? I did not see you at all. Have you no better sense than to dash out in front of a galloping horse?" The man's voice carried the force of one accustomed to having others jump at his bidding. His tone immediately raised her hackles. She tensed as he continued, "Are you hurt? And what the devil are you doing out here alone?" He looked around as though expecting another person to pop out of the thicket.

"One might better ask if you, sirrah, have no better sense than to gallop like a madman along a quiet country lane," Sarah retorted, still in the ditch, but not the least intimidated by his towering above her. "What's more, I have a perfect right to be here."

She started to pick herself up, then gasped as pain shot into her ankle. Her foot slipped and she would have fallen again had the stranger not moved to catch her in his arms.

"Here. Let me help you." He set her down on the edge of the road and ran his hand impersonally, but expertly over the outside of her footwear. Too stunned by his audacity to object to the impropriety of his touch, she accepted his examination.

"I must remove the boot to determine if there are broken bones," he said, tacitly asking her permission to do so as he crouched in the ditch at her feet and removed his gloves. She nodded her approval, biting her lip, and making no sound but a sharp intake of breath as he removed the boot.

Despite her pain, she noted a crop of light brown, not quite curly hair and a pair of entrancing gray eyes. His hands were warm and sensitive. An electrifying shock of emotion swept through her as he looked up at her. His eyes held hers for a long interval. Then she felt a warm blush suffuse her features.

"It is not broken, but I daresay you have a bad sprain," he said. "I will see you home safely. I assume you live near here? I saw a cottage over there." He pointed in the direction from which she had come.

"I live at Rosemont Manor, she said, trying unsuccessfully to insert her foot in the boot.

"And you are allowed to roam about so freely?" He pulled his gloves back on. "A young woman should have at least a maid or a groom accompany her when she goes jaunting about the countryside."

Now she was embarrassed. He thought she was a servant! She noted his buckskin breeches, boots that been exquisitely polished before his descent into the ditch, a linen shirt, stylish cravat, and black broadcloth coat. Even had her gown been clean, its age would hardly have recommended the wearer as a woman entitled to the respect due a member of the Quality. Embarrassment and amusement warred within her.

Amusement won out.

"As to that," she said, "the mistress of Rosemont would just as likely be out here alone herself."

"Really?" He raised an eyebrow skeptically.

She liked the warmth in those gray eyes. He was an extraordinarily attractive man, though not prettily handsome in the usual sense. His brows were well-defined, his lashes thick, his nose straight and well-shaped. He had high cheekbones, a firm chin, and a generous mouth. The only blemish she noted was a scar along his right cheek in an inverted "V" shape. Catching herself staring, she looked away. This had to be one of the gentlemen from Markhome Hall, but was it Markholme himself?

She knew she should disclose her identity, but the normally unflappable Miss Longbourne was uncertain, embarrassed, flustered—and feeling at a distinct disadvantage. So she held back.

"Oh, yes, really," she babbled. "Though in the normal course of events, she might be riding instead of walking."

"Lesser beings cannot expect to ride, eh?"

"Oh, I could have had a mount. I preferred to walk this morning." It was not a lie. Deceptive, but not a lie.

"We had better get you back to care for this sprain." He swept her into his arms with little effort and strode toward the waiting stallion. He settled her on the saddle with both her feet hanging near the left stirrup and started to mount behind her.

"My basket."

He retrieved the basket and handed it to her, along with her boot, and swung up behind her.

Reaching around her, he caught up the reins and urged the stallion into action. Encircled in his arms as she was, Sarah was very much aware of his body near her and equally aware that this situation was not proper. She held herself stiffly, trying not to touch him, but finding, when she could not avoid doing so, the sensation was not unpleasant.

"Relax," he said softly at her ear. "I am not going to carry you off to my cave just yet. You are making it difficult for Achilles to balance our weight. Just tell me where to go." She indicated the direction with a gesture, seriously fearing his warm breath on her neck had taken her voice away.

The gait of the horse bounced her leg, each bounce producing a jolt of pain. She concentrated on not crying out. She shifted her position slightly closer to him and he braced her with an arm around her waist. What must he think of her? She was grateful for his help, but after all, he was at fault, was he not? Moreover, there was a degree

of impertinence in his just taking charge as he had and
in his assumptions about the mistress of Rosemont.

"I am sure this must be painful for you," he said. "Try
to think of something else. Tell me about Rosemont. Do
you enjoy your position there?" His voice rose on the word
*position* as a question of just what her position was. She
ignored that, though, and with an occasional wince, she
told him of her home.

"Rosemont is a holding of just over six thousand acres—
rather modest in comparison with the Markholme lands,
but I happen to consider it very beautiful all the same.
The manor house itself dates from the time of Henry VIII.
It came to my g—to Lord Seaverton through his wife and
had been in her family since the sixteenth century." She
thought she sounded like a guide book.

"You seem very loyal." He spoke in polite neutrality.
"From what I have seen of the two holdings this morning,
Rosemont appears to be well managed. Miss Longbourne
must employ a very able man as steward."

"Well, her Mr. Howard is top-notch, but she makes all
the decisions." Sarah was miffed at the implied slight of
her own abilities. If this were, indeed, Markholme, he
might as well know at the outset what he was dealing with.
She gestured a change in direction.

"Really? One would hardly credit a lady of her status as
having the interest, let alone knowledge to manage a large
estate."

"Do you mean to say a woman could not handle the
task because it is more customary to find a male of the
species in that position?" She twisted in his arms to look
him in the eye. This action produced a severe twinge in
her ankle and a distinct flutter in her heart. She could not
tell which produced the small gasp.

He smiled, apparently amused at her vehemence.

"I fear you misinterpret, miss. I am merely surprised a
woman would take on such a masculine role. The women
I know are perfectly content to pursue feminine activities
and not encroach into gentlemen's business."

"What if a woman has a particular aptitude for something in what you call 'gentlemen's business'? Would you have her demur in using her abilities?"

"I cannot conceive what such aptitudes might be."

"Running an estate, for example."

" 'Twould be a most unusual activity for a woman."

"Do you believe running an estate is vastly different from directing a large household?"

"Having never actually done either, it is difficult for me to say. There must be some difference between the knowledge required in rotating crops or breeding stock and that necessary to counting linens or instructing cook on whether to serve partridge or quail on a given menu."

"But, as you say, your experience is perhaps limited," she said sweetly, gesturing the direction again.

Moments later, they came into Rosemont's stable yard where several members of her staff and her brother apparently awaited her arrival. Charles froze at the sight of his sister perched on a destrier in the arms of a stranger. Then he took a step toward them.

"Cook said you had gone off to the Johnsons, but we expected your return before this, Sarah."

"Oh, Miss Longbourne, we was that worrit about ye," cried Jeremy, the head stable boy, hurrying to take the basket from her.

Quickly dismounting, her escort reached to lift her from the saddle. His eyes met hers and he raised that skeptical eyebrow again as he instantly absorbed her name and position.

"Unfair," he murmured for her ears alone. "Decidedly unfair." But his eyes twinkled and she grinned at him impishly. Cradling her in his arms, he turned and said to the others, "There has been a slight mishap. Miss Longbourne has injured her ankle."

He carried her to the kitchen where a footman relieved him of his burden. Over the servant's shoulder she watched and listened as her brother thanked the stranger and introduced himself.

"And you are . . . ?" Charles prompted.

"Markholme." He offered Charles his hand and caught Sarah's eye to share a silent laugh with her. "I shall call tomorrow to inquire after Miss Longbourne, if I may." Then he was gone.

Well, well, well, Sarah mused as the footman conveyed her to her room followed by her maid. Not a very "agreeable" sort are you, Lord Markholme? But you are tolerable, I do believe. Quite tolerable, she thought, remembering the feel of his arms around her and forgetting, for the moment, her apprehension.

# Three

Leaving the Rosemont stables, Matthew chuckled. Round one goes to the lady. But damned if Trenville wasn't right about her not being such an antidote. Those eyes—were they blue or violet?—were fascinating, whether snapping in anger at being forced off the road, or clouded with pain, or twinkling in triumph over successfully hoodwinking him.

She was not the sort of woman he usually found attractive. She was scarcely of medium height; he preferred women tall and long of limb. An abundance of soft, brown curls surrounded an ordinary face. Ordinary—until she smiled, then it quite took one's breath away. But she was nothing at all like the coolly sophisticated blondes who normally caught his attention. He recalled lilac scent from her hair beneath his chin. She was well-proportioned, with generous curves—there had been a real flesh and blood woman under the harsh wool of that awful gown. And that was a well-turned ankle. He winced at the pun of that thought.

He had imagined Miss Longbourne to be a woman aware of her own consequence, someone with a mature, formal demeanor. Reality produced a woman who looked younger than her twenty-four or -five years. Another female might have swooned, thrown a tantrum, or seized upon the incident to exercise feminine coyness, but not this one. Where she might have been fearful and hysterical, she was trusting and practical.

He rejected the idea of being forced into parson's

mousetrap—even his choice of bride beyond his control—but things now seemed a shade less bleak than they had some hours earlier. And, after all, he *did* have a choice. He could refuse the title, stay with the army. And what? he asked himself scornfully. Think you can just ignore the responsibilities—and the opportunities—this land offers?

Everything hinged on obtaining adequate funding, though. Unfortunately, the only funding available came with a bride attached. Major Cameron had had no thought of marrying. The Earl of Markholme was being pushed into a grotesque caricature of the happiness a young lieutenant had once envisioned. That dismaying thought restored his original level of vexation.

Back at the Hall, his guests languished over the remains of their breakfast.

"You were out early this morning," Adrian noted. "What do you think of the state of the Markholme demesne, oh lord of the manor?"

"The small portion I saw is much the worse for neglect, despite some recent improvements."

"Well, you did say it was going to take an inordinate amount of effort and money to put it to rights," Adrian said.

"Uncle Arthur started to repair the damage, but he was hampered by a distinct lack of funds. And, he lost interest when his son died."

"Arthur Cameron was the second son—he inherited from his older brother? Is that right?" Adrian asked.

"Yes. When the first Matthew Cameron committed suicide. My father was the third son of the Fourth Earl. Father died when I was seven; Mother, five years later."

"Your family has had its share of troubles," Hendley observed.

Matthew nodded. "By rights I should never have come into the title at all."

"But you did—and the lands as well," Adrian said.

"Heavily encumbered lands." Matthew's tone was ironic,

then he brightened. "But my God! The possibilities are here, Adrian! Even I, unschooled as I am, can see them."

"Does this mean we are about to wish you happy?" Adrian drawled.

Matthew ignored the question. "Together Markholme and Rosemont control resources to support a sizable village—and be self-sustaining, I daresay. Markholme farms are sadly run down, though." He ran his hand through his hair in a characteristic gesture. "There is so much to be done!"

"Don't tell us there is a farmer beneath the military uniform you usually wear!"

Hendley picked up on the teasing tone of the marquis, "Who would have thought it? Here I charge over half of Europe following a dashing and courageous officer only to have him turn into a plodding farmer. You just never can tell."

"Oh, cut rope, you two." Matthew smiled as he helped himself from the sideboard and motioned to a footman to pour his coffee. "As soon as I finish here, you can go out with me and see for yourselves."

"Are we to meet your neighbors, Matthew? I own to interest in meeting particular members of local society."

Matthew knew exactly what Adrian meant.

"I plan to call at Rosemont tomorrow. After that . . ." He did not tell them he had met the mistress of Rosemont this morning. For now he would keep the memory of her laughing eyes and lively wit to himself.


The following afternoon, Matthew was ushered into a cheerful, well-appointed drawing room where he found the mistress of Rosemont seated in a wing chair, her injured foot propped on an ottoman. Putting aside a book she was reading, Sarah greeted him guardedly. Her dress, a blue print muslin, was properly modest, but did not conceal from his practiced eye a very satisfactory set of feminine curves. She was accompanied by a woman she introduced as her aunt Bess, a Mrs. Carstairs.

"Has the injury been very troublesome?" he asked. He stood looking down at her and held her proffered hand a shade longer than mere courtesy required.

"No, my lord." She smiled reassuringly, gazing at him through thick, dark lashes. "It was painful yesterday, but today it is fine as long as I put little pressure on it."

Still no feminine bid for sympathy and attention, he thought. He took the seat her aunt indicated. He was extraordinarily aware of the niece. The injury made her vulnerable, yet she seemed very much in command of her domain.

Aunt Bess noted politely that his visit was welcomed by local society. Soon Miss Longbourne's brother Charles joined them, eager to talk about the war and gratified to have firsthand information. To Matthew's surprise, Miss Longbourne took a lively interest in this topic.

"You both are remarkably well-informed about what is happening in the Peninsula," Matthew observed.

"We try to keep up on the news, don't we, Sarah? In the billiards room I have a map marked with battles. Perhaps you can help me make any necessary adjustments to it."

"Another time, Charles, please," his sister said. "He will drive one to distraction, my lord. He even has lead soldiers set up to simulate a major battle, and he knows the names of the leading officers of both our allies and the enemy!"

"Are you interested in a military career?" Matthew asked.

Before Charles could respond, the door opened and a petite feminine version of the young man all but bounced into the room.

"I hope I am not too late for tea. Oh," she said, catching sight of Matthew as he and Charles rose, "I beg your pardon."

"Emily, may I present Lord Markholme?" There was a trace of reproval in Sarah's voice. "I fear my sister is somewhat . . . enthusiastic, my lord."

The younger woman, in a sea green frock, offered Matthew her hand and a dazzling smile. Miss Longbourne is not the only beauty in the family, Matthew noted, and I would wager Miss Emily Longbourne could be a heartbreaker.

Charles cast Emily a reproachful glance as she and the gentlemen seated themselves. "To answer your question, sir—yes, I am very interested in a military career."

"Charles would give his right arm for a commission, my lord," Emily said. "Oh, dear. Then he would not be able to have one, would he? Oh, well. You can see his appreciation of things martial, I am sure."

"Yes, indeed," Matthew responded, "but we all have our special dreams or goals, do we not?"

"I suppose we do." Emily studied him for a moment. "You are not at all what we—that is, I—expected, my lord," she blurted.

Aunt Bess cleared her throat with a meaningful look at Emily. Charles rolled his eyes heavenward, and Matthew shared an amused glance with Sarah.

Over tea and lemon cakes, the conversation turned to the weather and prospects for good hunting. Markholme was invited to bring his guests to hunt in the Rosemont groves. When the tray was removed, Sarah must have given the others some unseen signal, for Aunt Bess politely excused herself and, ushering the other two out with her, left Sarah and Matthew rather improperly alone. Having risen as the other ladies left the room, he reseated himself in a chair nearer hers.

They stared at each other thoughtfully. Her eyes are definitely violet, he noted, and a man could drown in them. He felt an unfamiliar tightening of his body. She lowered her gaze first, and he made a slight noise deep in his throat.

"You must be aware that my intent in calling on you involves a good deal more than a polite inquiry about your injury," he started.

"Yes, I am." She paused a moment, then rushed on. "You and I, sir, are caught as puppets in a show that neither of us could have wished. One might almost say that your uncle and my grandfather are reaching from their graves to pull the strings."

"The imagery is appropriate, if somewhat uninviting." Matthew was relieved she would not be missish.

"I see no reason to wrap the truth in clean linen." Her eyes were dark with concern. Immediately, and without reasoning why, he wanted to comfort her. "Very honestly," she continued, "since Robert's death, I have had no real wish to marry, but I must do all in my power to protect the interests of my family."

"I see."

"There are, of course, many others on this estate—and on yours, as well—who will be directly affected by any course you and I may take."

"And you are ready to martyr yourself on the cross of matrimony. I am not sure I find that very flattering, Miss Longbourne." He felt an inexplicable twinge of annoyance at her affection for Robert. She had been in love with him, then.

"Now it is you who employ negative imagery. No, I did not mean to imply a sense of martyrdom. Nor did I think it necessary to flatter you. I assume your presence here indicates some interest in abiding by the terms of those two wills." Her voice rose to make the last statement a question.

"Yes. I am interested in at least exploring the possibilities they present. If I may be frank," he raised his brows questioningly and waited for her nod, "I find myself under a great deal of pressure to accept the conditions of those documents."

"I thought so. I, too, find I must accept the necessity of circumstances. And I think it imperative that we be thoroughly honest with each other from the very outset."

"As you were yesterday?" His grin lightened the mood.

"All right . . ." She looked a bit sheepish.

"I must confess that I expected this discussion to be much more difficult," he went on. "Since we are being so honest, let me tell you what I would expect from our union. Obviously, I must have funds—a veritable fortune is needed to make Markholme what it can be. It appears we both need those funds."

"True."

"If we fail to reach an agreement, the fortune goes elsewhere, does it not?"

"Yes. The bulk of the fortune and Rosemont would then go to the new Lord Seaverton, whom I have not met."

"Leaving you and yours quite out in the cold."

"Yes."

He rubbed his chin thoughtfully. "Even a cursory overview of things tells me that these two estates might be managed more expeditiously if they were combined."

"That was the plan of our string-pulling relatives. I would agree to such an arrangement, but I would ask that no person presently attached to Rosemont as servant or tenant be turned out without just cause."

"Would you accept your having sole power to dismiss anyone presently employed in any capacity on Rosemont, but we must agree on any new additions to personnel?"

She nodded.

"Have you other stipulations of a general nature?" he asked.

"Only what I have alluded to before—a commission for Charles with a suitable allowance as supplement, a season for Emily and a suitable marriage settlement when she weds, and that Aunt Bess be provided for."

"And for yourself?"

She colored slightly. "I believe I am provided for quite adequately in the detailed requirements of Grandpapa's will—if we accept his terms."

"I also have family to consider. I understand the parish church is currently under the temporary custody of a curate. Is this living not assigned at the discretion of the Earl of Markholme?"

"Yes, it is."

"I should like to see my sister's husband established in that position to bring my sister nearer," Matthew said. "He presently serves as vicar in a parish in Kent."

"Mr. Bascomb has long desired to remove to Sussex with a widowed daughter. He stayed on here so as not to leave us without a clergyman."

"Good. The perfect solution, then."

"Yes. May all our concerns be so easily dispensed with." She flashed him that devastating smile. "Was there anything else, my lord?"

"As a matter of fact, there is." He looked at her intently. "This is a somewhat delicate matter, but I feel we should be candid. I would not entertain the idea of what is politely termed a 'marriage of convenience.' I expect to exercise a husband's rights in the bedroom. It is, of course, necessary to secure the succession—and, at least until that goal is met, I would demand absolute fidelity from my wife."

She was quiet as she held his gaze, then she said, "May she make equal demands upon you, my lord?"

Her frankness surprised him, but he noted a becoming blush, too. *Could* she make equal demands? *Should* she? "Hmmm. Well. Umm." He groped for a response. "The situation is not precisely the same, is it, Miss Longbourne?"

"I am aware of the differences between the sexes, my lord, and, surprising as it may be, I even have some idea of the mating process and procreation." She seemed embarrassed, but determined to make her point. "My question has more to do with the social aspects of a marriage such as ours would likely be. I would not enjoy being an object of pity as gossips clucked over my husband's peccadilloes."

"I see. Peccadilloes are acceptable if one is discreet—is that it?"

"Well, no. I mean . . . perhaps . . . oh. I don't know exactly what I mean now." She waved her hand impatiently.

He laughed, not unkindly, amused at her confusion in contrast to her previous frankness. "We can perhaps deal with such an issue if and when it comes up. However—" His tone became serious. "I will give you this pledge: I would never willingly or knowingly subject my wife to public ridicule."

This seemed to mollify her, for she gave him a tentative

smile and he found himself ensnared by those intriguing eyes again.

"So? Are we agreed then?" he asked. When she nodded, he went on. "I know this is not the romantic proposal young girls dream of, but will you do me the honor of becoming my wife?"

"Yes." She looked him directly in the eye and she seemed as surprised as he at her lack of hesitation. "But could we wait a while before making a public announcement? I will inform my family, of course, but could we take a few days? We are constrained by circumstances, but I should like to put a little better face on it, if we may."

"As you wish, Miss Longbourne." Taking her hand, he brushed his lips against her fingers. He was touched by her honesty, by her resolve, and by that feminine need to "put a better face on it." It bespoke vulnerability that again aroused a sense of protectiveness in him.

He left soon afterward, promising to dine at Rosemont two evenings hence. He was to bring his house guests as well to meet some of the local gentry.

It is done, he thought, as he returned to his own estate, and much more quickly than he had anticipated. Also—thanks to the character of the woman who would be his wife—with more dignity and grace than he had expected. He tried to think of improvements that would be possible on his own property now. He tried to consider the precise steps to finish his obligation to his regiment and give up his commission. Instead, conflicting scenes kept intruding. He could not put from his mind the image of a small woman with laughing eyes and a sense of honor equal to any he had encountered on the battlefield.

But neither could he forget that she was the daughter of the woman who jilted his uncle and sent him down the road to destruction. Wasn't there some adage about the acorn not falling far from the tree? Nor could he forget that once before he had trusted a woman only to have his dreams turn to dust.

At least his heart was not engaged this time.

# Four

Sarah's ankle pain had diminished to an occasional twinge, but it was not physical discomfort that distracted her from estate duties. She was betrothed! To a man whose dark attractiveness and disturbingly masculine body occupied her sleeping and wakeful hours to a degree she would have found incredible only days earlier. The proposal had been offered and accepted in an almost businesslike manner, but a distinct physical charge had jolted through her when his lips brushed her fingers. Strength and controlled power—the man wore them like shining armor, but she sensed depth to these qualities.

Good heavens! What is the matter with me? I never reacted so with Robert—and we shared real kisses! It must be tension—and the strange circumstances. Silly romantic notions were out of the question. This marriage was a contract to secure the future of two estates.

Surprising her maid by her attention to dressing on the evening of the planned dinner, she settled on a lavender gown of watered silk. With it, she wore an amethyst pendant and matching earrings. Her short dark hair curled becomingly around her face.

"You look splendid," Emily cried as she met Sarah in the hall. "Lord Markholme will surely be captivated."

"You are looking very nice yourself, little sister."

Emily's gold gown with brown trim set off her honey-colored hair and brown eyes perfectly. A gold topaz brooch on a brown ribbon graced her neck.

"Do you think Jonathan Wilkes will notice me now?" Emily asked, twirling in front of her audience of one.

"I think, you silly girl, that Jonathan Wilkes could hardly take his eyes off you the last time we met him and you were dressed in deepest mourning then!"

Jonathan had been Emily's dance partner at several assemblies before the Longbournes' social activities were curtailed by Lord Seaverton's illness. This was to be their first entertainment since his death. To meet the new Earl of Markholme, they had invited James Wilkes, a local baron, with his wife and son; Squire Compson and his wife; and the dowager Countess Meridon and her daughter Sybil. Sir William Denton—knighted some years earlier—along with his wife and their daughter Delia rounded out the local guests.

Assembled in the main drawing room, the family welcomed their first guests, the party from Markholme Hall. Sarah caught her breath at the sight of Matthew in evening finery. He cast an appreciative eye on her own raiment, and she knew all the fuss about dressing for dinner had been worth it.

Introductions accomplished all around, Sarah observed with amusement the handsome, amiable Lieutenant Hendley was likely to put Jonathan Wilkes in the shade. The lieutenant was an immediate hit with the younger Longbournes.

As the three younger people engaged in conversational pleasantries, Trenville turned to Aunt Bess, noting that her late husband had been one of his father's school chums. These diversions allowed Sarah and Matthew a private moment.

"You are looking in especially fine form this evening," he said.

"Thank you, my lord. One could say the same of you."

"I assume you informed your family of our plans?" She nodded and he continued, "I wrote my sister—and shared

the news with Trenville and Hendley this morning. You
may have perceived that Trenville is the brother I never
had."

"Having a friend to confide in is one of life's most precious treasures," she said with a touch of melancholy.
"Robert was such a friend to me. I miss sharing things
with him. We used to laugh a good deal." She smiled up
at him as he gave her hand a quick squeeze. She felt a
warm glow at the physical contact.

Lofton announced the Wilkes family's entrance, followed by the arrival of the rest of the guests. In the flurry
of new introductions, Sarah and Matthew separated.

As guest of honor, though, Matthew escorted her in to
dinner and was seated on her right. He was politely attentive to her and to Mrs. Compson on his other side. Intensely aware of him, Sarah marveled that she herself
could deal in such banalities and she wondered if he felt
as tense as she did.

Conversation flowed smoothly over a dinner prepared
perfectly with several removes. At one point Sarah intercepted a silent communication from Trenville to Markholme. The marquis raised his glass in a subtle salute with
a smile that included both Matthew and Sarah. When the
ladies withdrew to the drawing room, Sarah leaned over
her brother's shoulder to whisper a reminder not to allow
the gentlemen to linger overlong with their port.

In the drawing room, the younger girls of the party com-
pared notes on the eligible gentlemen. The three newcomers were all deemed acceptable, with Trenville having the
edge in wealth and position and Hendley the advantage
in looks. For once, Sarah noted, Emily was forced to keep
her own counsel.

Mrs. Compson and Aunt Bess, friends of long standing,
engaged Lady Wilkes in a comfortable coze. The dowager
Countess Meridon, tall and spare, rarely let others forget
she was the highest ranking woman of the district. She
took great pains to keep abreast of who was who in the
pages of Burke's guide to the peerage. She sat very straight

on the edge of her chair and subtly, but pointedly let others appreciate her condescension in conversing politely with Lady Denton, wife of a mere knight.

Sarah usually found Lady Meridon's social games amusing, but she settled herself near Lady Denton to protect that dear woman from the dowager's poisoned darts. Lady Meridon had long ago discovered Miss Longbourne to be simply immune to social pretensions, though the dowager Countess Meridon would never have labeled a proper regard for titles and consequence as *pretension*. Oh, my, no.

Lady Denton made a polite comment about the manners of the Marquis of Trenville.

"You know, of course, he is heir to a dukedom." The dowager Lady Meridon's tone indicated she was smugly certain her listeners did *not* know. "Therefore, as the daughter of an earl, my Sybil is the only lady in the room truly eligible for either the marquis or the earl."

"Sometimes the heart fails to take note of Burke's, does it not, Lady Meridon?" Sarah's smile took the sting out of her question.

"Those who stray from their own station in choosing a mate invariably court disaster," Lady Meridon responded firmly. "Your own mother is a case in point, dear Sarah."

"I beg your pardon." Sarah withheld a gasp.

"She might have married the fifth Earl of Markholme, you know. Had she done so, your brother would be the earl now. But she chose instead the second son of a mere baron, thus bringing catastrophe on all of them, not to mention leaving her children with little real standing."

"She saved herself being married to a drunken gamester," Sarah said tartly, "and she was very happy with her choice."

" 'Tis known your parents were very devoted to each other," Lady Denton said tentatively.

"Devotion, Lady Denton, has little to do with fulfilling one's duty to family and society. Indulging in romantic

nonsense is no way to preserve our civilized society." The
dowager's voice was shrill and dogmatic.

Sarah and Lady Denton shared a glance, then shrugged
their shoulders. The whole county knew there had been
little romantic nonsense in the late Lord Meridon's life
and he had sought solace elsewhere. Before either could
reply, the gentlemen rejoined the ladies.

Jonathan Wilkes, a veritable pink of the *ton* in a lime
green jacket over a rose brocade vest and white breeches,
took a position near Emily and posed quite grandly for
the assemblage. Sarah thought he truly did resemble the
tulip to which such would-be Corinthians were often com-
pared. She fought back a smile, but her lips twitched when
Markholme caught her eye as he, too, observed the young
man.

Lady Meridon maneuvered the Marquis of Trenville into
a discussion with her daughter, then dominated the conversation herself with coy questions to Trenville about his-
father-the-duke and mention of other high-ranking names.
Then she turned to Matthew.

"You know, Lord Markholme, the countess Poindexter
is my niece? I think you knew her during her season. She
was Miss Dalrymple then, of course—and quite the belle
of that season."

Lady Meridon's voice carried and Sarah, speaking with
the Dentons and Squire Compson, glanced at Matthew.
He seemed to tense momentarily, then responded politely.

"Yes. Miss Dalrymple conquered the social world that
year," he said in a neutral tone.

"Indeed." Trenville interjected smoothly. "She broke
all our hearts, just as I imagine this young lady is in a fair
way of doing. I understand you are to be presented this
season, Lady Sybil?"

"Oh, yes, I am, my lord, and I am looking forward to it
immensely." Lady Sybil, by no means an antidote, but no
raving beauty either, was flattered to be so singled out for
his attention.

Her mother was not to be put off so easily by Trenville's

diversion. Her next remark seemed directed to the room at large.

"The Poindexters and Dalrymples accepted my invitation to spend the Christmas season here. They arrive in a week's time and I plan a gala ball for them. Derbyshire does not offer the sort of company one is used to in London," she said disparagingly, "but we shall contrive, I make no doubt."

Sarah saw a look of understanding and sympathy pass between Trenville and his friend. Matthew glanced at her with an enigmatic expression. She smiled at him uncertainly and turned back to her own discussion, but that brief look troubled her. What did it mean?

Squire Compson rescued the evening from the domination of Lady Meridon by calling for Emily to treat them to some music. Emily was an accomplished and talented musician. Where another young woman not long out of the schoolroom might have been shy and awkward as the focus of so much attention, she was poised and in her element. She began with an intricate piece by Mozart followed by one from Handel. The others applauded as she finished.

"The concert is over. Come, Charles." She beckoned to her brother. "Join me at this instrument—and the rest of you must lend us your voices—or your ears as you please."

Charles proved to be adept, though somewhat less talented than his sister. Obviously, the two often played together and enjoyed doing so. They laughed over a minor blunder or two, but kept on playing a medley of country songs and ballads.

Sarah, standing very close to Matthew, felt the warmth of his arm touching hers and she caught that special masculine scent she remembered from their ride the other day. She started to move away slightly, but with his body and her dress shielding the movement from others in the room, he caught her little finger in his own to hold her near. She glanced up to see a teasing twinkle in his eye.

The group around the pianoforte might have gone on

at great length, had Sarah not caught Aunt Bess's signal that the entertainment had run its course for the older guests. The party broke up shortly afterward.

Charles invited the men to join a hunting expedition the next day. Markholme begged off, for he and Sarah planned to discuss estate matters and a wedding.

Twenty minutes after the last guest departed, Emily, readied for bed, virtually skipped into Sarah's room as Sarah completed her own preparations to retire. Emily had just settled herself cross-legged in the middle of Sarah's bed when Aunt Bess joined them, followed by Charles, who first ascertained that the ladies were suitably covered.

"I thought the evening went very well," Aunt Bess observed to general agreement.

"You know," Emily said, "the earl grows on one, does he not? He is really quite an amiable sort, though he is more reserved than the marquis or Lieutenant Hendley."

Charles gave an exaggerated sigh. "Of course he is. After all, he's a soldier, a commander of dozens of men. Trenville is a diplomat and Hendley is only a junior officer. Lieutenants ain't required to do much thinking."

"Lieutenant Hendley is a cut above most," Emily argued. "He comes from a family of soldiers. His grandfather was a general in the war in the colonies and his father is serving in India. His family is there also."

"Uh, oh!" Charles grinned. "Poor Jonathan is losing out, I fear. And he was dressed so prettily tonight, too. He probably chose each item of his apparel just to impress you, Emily, and what did you do? You spent the evening flirting with the handsome soldier boy."

"I did *not*. I was not at all untoward in my behavior, was I, Sarah? Aunt Bess?"

"No, no. Of course not. Charles just likes to tease," Sarah assured her. "I was grateful to both of you. Your music was quite the hit of the evening."

"Are you firmly resolved to have the earl as a husband, Sarah?" Charles asked. "I mean, nothing has been announced yet—you can cry off, if you've a mind to."

Aware that Charles had been quietly watching her and the earl all evening, Sarah was sure he asked the question all three wanted to put to her.

"Charles has a point," Aunt Bess said. "Once it is made public, the scandal would be rather horrible if you changed your mind."

"Oh, Sarah, we do want you to be happy," Emily added.

"I am content with the decision," Sarah said. "I gave my word. I could hardly go back on it now. Nor do I wish to do so. I think this whole affair may turn out more agreeably than we anticipated."

"He seems a fine man," Aunt Bess said.

"Top drawer," Charles agreed.

"And quite good-looking." Emily grinned.

"And on that inane note, let us all get some rest." Sarah shooed them out with a hug for each.

She lay awake for some time, though, considering her reactions to the sheer masculinity of this man she had agreed to marry. *I am in a fair way to making a fool of myself, I fear. This is a business arrangement. Lady Meridon is a frightful snob, but she has the right of it in not assigning much credence to romantic nonsense. Still . . . Mama and Papa were inordinately happy in their romantic nonsense. So was Aunt Bess. But it cannot be a consideration for me.*

*Can it?*

# Five

Sarah might have taken comfort in knowing that Matthew, too, found sleep elusive. He thought her a capable hostess and easy conversationalist, making everyone feel welcomed and important, even that harridan, Lady Meridon. Knowing himself reserved in society, he reasoned that this quality enhanced her recommendations as his wife.

In tabulating her positive qualities, he tried not to dwell on the scent of lilac which he already associated with her, or the enticing swell of bosom in a lace-edged neckline, or that the briefest of touches aroused a desire for more.

Matthew had not spent his adult years living like a monk, but since the debacle with Annalisa, he had confined his amorous activities to members of the demimonde. He aimed for little emotional involvement. That goal should not be impossible in a marriage that was essentially a business deal. Clearly, theirs would not be the romantic idyll he had once dreamed of for himself and the woman he loved. Love. Thank God, love had no part of this arrangement. Once bitten, twice shy, he reminded himself.

With this thought he remembered that Annalisa Dalrymple—that is, Poindexter—would be in the area soon. It was unlikely he could avoid meeting her here—or in the city. For one thing, her husband wielded considerable influence in Parliament—the political arena the new Lord Markholme would enter. For another, in a country district, one was apt to see the same people repeatedly at social functions.

The next day, in buckskin breeches and a jacket of dark blue broadcloth, and armed with his own estate books, he presented himself at Rosemont after the hunters had departed. Coming from behind the massive desk in the library, Sarah extended her hand in greeting.

"We shall work here where we can both see what we are about." She indicated a large, heavy, antique table on which lay an open dictionary and an atlas they pushed aside to make room for the ledgers. "I'll ask Lofton to bring more tea. Tea always makes work go more smoothly."

As they settled down to the tasks they had set for themselves, Matthew was acutely aware of her body near his.

"Let us deal with the wedding first, then see which functions of our two estates might most expediently be combined," he suggested.

They set a wedding date between Christmas and the new year. The hardships of winter travel dictated a small affair. There would be only family and local guests, though Trenville would return to act as witness, along with Emily.

"Will that give you enough time to prepare?" Matthew asked.

"Yes, my lord. I do not envision an elaborate trousseau."

"Do you think we might get so very personal now, Sarah, as to use our Christian names?"

"Why yes, M—Matthew. I think we might, though I am sure the Lady Meridons of the world would not approve."

"Luckily, we can ignore their strictures." Reverting to the question of time, he added, his tone more serious, "Sarah, I regret the haste, but I must return to the continent. I gave my word. And the wedding must take place soon to meet the requirements set forth in those wills. Both our interests will be taken care of then, in the event something should happen to me."

"When do you expect to leave us?"

"Wellington wants me there prior to engaging the French on their own soil. Hendley and I will be taking dispatches to him from the foreign office—whenever those august gentlemen can make up their ponderous minds as to what it is they want in those dispatches." His was the impatient tone of a man of action forced into the limbo of waiting.

"In other words, you—we—cannot be certain?"

"You have the right of it, my dear. We even have to postpone a proper wedding journey, for I must be on hand when those dispatches are ready. I promise to make it up to you once we have managed to 'dispatch' Boney himself."

"The sooner, the better." She flashed him a quick smile, but left him wondering whether she referred to a wedding journey or to Bonaparte's dispatchment.

Other details of the wedding were accomplished in short order.

"I wonder if we shall so readily agree when we turn to matters of the estates as we do on the wedding," Sarah mused aloud.

"Let us hope so, but it is probably inevitable that we disagree eventually."

And, sure enough, they did.

Matthew's time in London clubs had not centered on gaming and drinking. He had developed a friendship with Samuel Whitbread, an older man whose fortune came from the brewery business. Having now familiarized himself with the local resources, Matthew thought a small brewery might become a going concern in Derbyshire.

Sarah, too, had given thought to the establishment of new industry. The district needed employment for an increasing number of people. Her proposal, however, was to install a pottery manufactory. A huge deposit of clay spreading across their two holdings provided a ready source of the basic requirement for pottery.

Each argued at length regarding the market appeal of the particular product. Matthew insisted it would be easier to train people for work in a brewery than for pottery-making. Sarah said pottery would create more jobs.

In the end, they agreed on two things. First, new industry offered a means to help people help themselves. Sarah impressed her prospective husband when she mentioned that the end of the war was certain to bring a multitude of returning soldiers seeking jobs. He knew few army officers, let alone members of Parliament, who had such foresight. Second, they agreed to gather and share more information before they made a final decision.

Privately, Matthew could not decide whether to admire Sarah's business acumen, or to be irritated that she did not bend more readily to his superior masculine insight. No other woman of his acquaintance would have argued this issue, persistently defending her position in the face of firm opposition from a man. No. Most women of his acquaintance dealt with resistance by pouting, cajoling, whining, or crying. Not this one, though.

A more heated clash came over the question of managing the extraordinarily large holding that Rosemont and Markholme, combined, would create. Military strategist that he was, Matthew admitted to being out of his element in this regard. He proposed they find a man with experience and good credentials to take over general management.

"You realize, Sarah, I may be gone for quite some time. I should like to feel things were being handled properly. With a man to oversee the whole endeavor, Ainsley and Howard could carry on the duties of specific management. Our common interests would be well cared for."

She stiffened next to him.

"Matthew, you seem to have very little opinion of my abilities." Anger overrode the hurt in her voice. "Grandpapa and I were virtually partners in the management of this estate and since his death I have done quite well on my own, thank you very much!"

"Be reasonable, Sarah. Rosemont is not even a third the size of Markholme. The task of management will be monumental when the holdings are one." Matthew was used to giving orders, not negotiating.

"Yes, Rosemont is less than a third the size of Markholme, but acre for acre, it is twice as productive! Now, how do you suppose that came to be, my lord?"

"Matthew," he said quietly. "My name is Matthew. Or Matt, if you prefer. Look, Sarah, I was only trying to make things easier. You just said you merely assisted your grandfather and surely since his death you have done little but continue the measures he initiated."

"I said we were partners." He heard the irritation deepen in her voice. "Grandpapa respected my opinion. He often discussed his proposals with me, as well as with Mr. Howard—and certain of our tenants whose views he valued. True—in the last few months we have initiated little that is new, but projects that are in place are those Grandpapa and I worked out together."

Lord, would she never see the folly of what she was suggesting? The idea of a woman commanding an army of tenant farmers and cottage workers as well as running two or three households was preposterous.

"You have not forgotten, have you," he asked patiently, "that you will be managing a much larger staff at Markholme than you have had to deal with at Rosemont? In fact, your domestic responsibilities will probably extend to Rosemont as well as Markholme Hall and the London town house."

"Aunt Bess has always taken an active role in the running of Rosemont. And Emily has some understanding of household management. I see no reason for them not to take a greater role—that is if they continue to live under our protection?" This ended as an apprehensive question.

"Of course they will." Now *he* was getting a little testy. "How could you think otherwise?"

"Well, then, I think you are looking for difficulty where none need exist," she said confidently. "I ran the Rosemont household and Grandpapa's town house. I also helped him run the estate. Size notwithstanding, I see very little difference in the nature of the duties I would have after our marriage and those I perform now."

"The kinds of duties may be similar, but the volume is not. I cannot have you bearing such a burden."

"It *will* be a great deal of work," she conceded, "but it will not be forever, will it? You do plan to return to England, do you not? At which time I assume you will accept a fair share of the responsibilities."

"I am trying—apparently without success—to accept responsibility now by hiring a man to act as my surrogate in estate matters."

"A man."

"Yes. Someone to see to the overall management."

"When you have a perfectly capable manager right here who just happens to be female."

"I do not want you to do this, Sarah." He looked directly into her eyes, his stern expression one that had effectively cowed junior officers. "Nor do I think this is what your grandfather had in mind with his will."

"Are you forbidding me to do so?" Her own expression was unreadable.

"Would you cry off the marriage if I did?"

She became very still. With only a slight pause and her voice firm, she responded. "No. I gave you my word. But— I would be disappointed. And hurt."

"I am not forbidding you," he said slowly, "but I repeat: I do not wish you to take on all this responsibility alone."

"I understand your concern, Matthew." Her conciliatory tone eased the tension. "Yes, it would be better were you able to be here. Heaven knows absentee landlords can be disastrous for a region."

"With my wife in residence, I could hardly be considered an absentee landlord." He was stung by her words. "Estate management is simply not something one leaves up to a woman."

"Why?"

"What do you mean 'why'? It just isn't."

"That is not a reason."

"How about this, then: I do not want my wife doing the work a man should be doing. Even if I were here, I would have a capable man assist me until I learned the ropes. I cannot expect you to do my job."

"Please, Matthew, allow me to try." She impulsively put her hand on his. She was pleading now, but quietly and forthrightly, with no feminine tears or hysterics. She seemed to have no idea what those violet eyes were doing to his determination and defenses, or how the warmth of her hand bolted through his body. "I know I can do this," she said. "Let me prove it to you."

"How?" He felt himself weakening.

"I am a competent manager. I will send you detailed reports while you are away. If at any time you sincerely feel our interests are being mismanaged, I will accede to your wishes to hire an overseer steward."

"And when I return?"

"We will work together—unless you want me to do it all." That impish sparkle had returned to her eyes.

"All right." His reluctance hung thick in the air between them. "I cannot like this decision and I accept only under the conditions you have stated."

"Thank you," she said softly. "I promise you will not be disappointed."

"Ah, woman, you have beaten me down," he said, putting his arm around her shoulder and drawing her closer. "Adam never had a chance, did he?"

She was softness and strength combined in his embrace. He had been intensely conscious of her ever since they sat down. His leg touching hers caused sparks of desire. As she reached for one of the ledgers or a piece of paper, her breast had grazed his arm, turning mere sparks into full blown flames. She turned toward him, their eyes locking. Slowly, giving her time to withdraw if she wanted to, he lowered his mouth to hers.

Her lips soft and pliant against his, she responded to him tentatively. He deepened the kiss. At first she seemed reluctant, then she opened to him and with a low moan he tasted the full of her sweet mouth. Finally, regaining control of himself, he pulled away slightly.

"And you say *Adam* never had a chance," she whispered, apparently shaken.

He grinned and kissed her lightly again.

# Six

His estate demanded Matthew's attention in the next few days. Guest rooms were prepared for his sister and her family—due to arrive in a fortnight. Renovation of the Hall—sorely needed after years of neglect—would wait until Sarah was established as mistress.

He, Trenville, and Hendley visited frequently at Rosemont. One afternoon, Charles suggested a game of billiards. Emily and Sarah joined them.

Besides a billiards table at one end of a large room, there were smaller tables for card games. Decoration of the room included tapestry wall hangings and Charles' map of military campaigns on the Iberian Peninsula. A diorama complete with miniature lead figures painted to represent British, French, Spanish, and Portuguese soldiers depicted the Battle of Vitoria. Charles was pleased, but slightly embarrassed as the two veterans of that battle praised his accuracy.

On a small table set between two wing chairs in front of the fireplace, an exquisite ivory and ebony chess set invited play.

"Who is the chess player?" asked Trenville, picking up one of the pieces.

"Sarah is currently our champion," said Charles proudly. "She had lots of practice during Grandfather's illness, so I should beware of her, were I you."

"I sense a challenge in that remark," Trenville said, smiling. "Miss Longbourne, will you honor me with a game?"

"I should be happy to, my lord, but only if you call me Sarah."

"Fine. And you must call me Adrian, for I feel we are sure to become good friends."

Charles turned to his younger sister. "All right, Emily, that means you will have to play billiards so our sides are even. You can team with me."

"I think I should rather be partnered by Lieutenant Hendley," Emily declared. Hendley's expression was a comical mixture of delight and dismay. He probably thinks she knows nothing about the game, Sarah thought. She smiled at Adrian.

"Our young soldier is in for a surprise, I think," she whispered as they placed themselves at the chessboard.

Charles's pride in his sisters was well-placed, for both acquitted themselves ably in games held to be primarily masculine pursuits. Emily flirted and teased, but she took the game seriously and demonstrated such expertise that she nearly outshone her partner. He was surprised, but pleased when they narrowly defeated the earl and her brother.

Settling into their own game, Sarah and Adrian managed to shut out the frivolity from the other end of the room.

"Charles had the right of it, Sarah. You do have a commendable mastery of this game," Adrian said, as he tried to maneuver his queen out of a tight spot. "You and Matthew will be well matched."

"I hope so." She paused in her play to look at him directly. "I do hope so."

"He is my friend, so I am biased, of course, but he is a good and honorable man, Sarah. He will do right by you."

"He commands your loyalty, Adrian. That speaks volumes for him, I am sure."

Their own game over, the billiards foursome came to watch. Sarah caught a sympathetic smile from Matthew as she was forced into a move that would inevitably give the game to Trenville.

"Nicely done, Adrian. I shall expect a rematch some time," she said, as they all moved to the drawing room to join Aunt Bess for tea.

Good-natured rehashing of the games was interrupted when Lofton presented a message on a salver. Sarah recognized Lady Meridon's seal.

"Lady Meridon's guests will arrive early in the week. She plans a ball for next Saturday evening." Sarah looked up from the note to observe a puzzling look pass between Adrian and Matthew.

"Is our young friend in danger of losing his heart?" Adrian asked as he and Matthew lingered over the remains of breakfast. Hendley had just departed for an excursion with the younger Longbournes.

"Lord, I hope not. Emily is a lovely girl, but she does not seem enamored of one Richard Hendley. She flirts with you, me, young Wilkes—even her brother—as much as with Hendley."

"She is a charmer, all right, but she seems to stay within the bounds of propriety."

"True. I hope he has not formed an attachment there. I should hate to see another young lieutenant laid low by the wiles of a lovely blonde."

"Which brings to mind the Meridon ball and the presence of the incomparable Annalisa. You *are* planning to attend, are you not?"

"Yes. I will eventually live in this district—it would not do to offend a neighbor, even that one. Besides, if I refused, I would have to explain to Sarah why I did not wish to attend the affair."

"Will some explanation not be required anyway?"

"Why? My relationship with Lady Poindexter is a thing of the past. There is no reason for Sarah to know of it. Not that it should matter to her at all."

Adrian looked at him dubiously. "Trust me. It will matter if it comes to her through the gossip mill."

"This is not a love match, Adrian. Sarah and I accept the alliance as a means of furthering our mutual financial interests. There is no need for us to become involved in each other's romantic past. Some things are best left alone."

"As you will, my friend. As you will." Adrian did not sound convinced.

In truth, Matthew was less convinced than he managed to appear. Certainly he intended the alliance to be as he had described it, but he was eager to know his prospective bride better on a purely personal level. As their acquaintance grew, he made little discoveries about her that intrigued him—a tendency to pull at a strand of hair when she concentrated, the way her lips tightened in determination, her inclination to tilt her head in confusion, and the controlled energy and grace with which she moved.

There had been no more passionate kisses, though there were often occasions for casual touches. Who could say he deliberately manufactured more of these occasions than could be strictly casual? He thought—he hoped—she felt the same inklings of desire he experienced.

Inexplicable spasms of jealousy hit him when she spoke of Robert. What kind of mawkish schoolboy reaction was this? He was not pleased to find he chided himself more often than he would have imagined possible.

When the Markholme party visited Rosemont one afternoon, Sarah asked to speak privately with Matthew. He followed her to the library.

"What is it?" he asked. "You look upset."

She gestured to the table strewn with account books—hers and those he had left the other day. "There is something very wrong here, Matthew. I have been over these books myself twice and this morning I asked Mr. Howard to review them, too."

"And . . . ?"

"We think Mr. Ainsley has been regularly stealing from your estate."

"What? Are you sure? That is a serious charge."

"See for yourself, please." She pointed to given items. "There is a sharp difference between figures that should appear here and those that do."

"How did you discover this? The books *seem* to be in order."

"Certain transactions should have been the same in both sets of books. When they were not, I looked more closely."

He studied the entries for several minutes. Finally, he looked up. "It was cleverly done, was it not?"

"Very cleverly done. And over a long period of time."

"Ainsley has been robbing Markholme for years!"

They dispatched a Rosemont footman immediately to notify Mr. Ainsley to meet his employer at Markholme Hall later that day.

The agent, dressed neatly in a manner befitting a country squire, presented himself as instructed.

"Sit down, please," Matthew said.

Removing his hat, Ainsley sat and glanced nervously at the open account books on the earl's desk. "Somethin' amiss, my lord?"

"I would say something is very much amiss, Ainsley," Matthew said, plunging right in. "I hope you have a logical explanation for the discrepancies in your recordings of certain items here."

"Are you accusing me of wrongdoing, my lord?" Ainsley blustered. "I ain't done nothin' wrong. I been serving this estate for near eight years now. Ain't had no complaints before."

"You have been systematically stealing from this estate for at least seven of those eight years," Matthew said emphatically. "The proof is irrefutable when you compare our books to those of Rosemont."

"I don't know about Rosemont business. Got nothin' to do with me."

"It does now." Matthew looked at him directly, but Ainsley refused to meet his eyes. "I have no choice but to dismiss you. I will not call in the magistrate, but neither will I provide you a reference. You are to be off Markholme land and out of the district by the end of the week."

"You got no call to do this. Whoever says I done wrong is lyin'. It was that meddlin' woman at Rosemont, wasn't it?"

"That is enough." Matthew's voice resounded with the authority of one accustomed to being obeyed without question. "The decision is final."

"You got no call," Ainsley repeated and picked up his hat. "No call a'tall. An' without a reference? You ain't heard the last of Gerald Ainsley."

The Rosemont residents looked forward with subdued eagerness to the Meridon ball. Sarah was also somewhat apprehensive. Although their betrothal would not be formally announced for several days yet, this was the first time she and Matthew would appear in public together.

Again she was inordinately conscious of her appearance and dress as she prepared for the evening. She finally chose a favorite gown from last season, a simply designed dark green velvet trimmed with touches of white fur.

"Do you suppose Lady Meridon will allow the waltz?" Emily asked as their carriage drove the few miles to the Meridon estate. "I hope so. I do love to waltz."

"I should not be surprised if the lady has included more than one waltz in the evening's offerings," Sarah said, recalling Lady Meridon's less than subtle designs on the Marquis of Trenville.

"The waltz is terribly risqué," Aunt Bess said, "but I must admit that were I your age, Emily, I should like it immensely." She heaved an exaggerated sigh. "However, being of the dowager generation now, I must purse my lips and frown disapprovingly."

They all laughed companionably.

After a while, Charles asked, "Do you know Lady Meridon's guests? I think there was a Dalrymple at Harrow when I was there."

"Lady Dalrymple was a distant cousin of my dear Freddie," Aunt Bess answered, "and we lived in the same district for many years. I look forward to seeing her again."

"Robert and his father spoke of Lord Poindexter," Sarah said. "Grandpapa knew him, too. I believe he is a member of the racing set—a well-known horse breeder. His stables are quite famous."

"And he married the Dalrymple daughter?" Emily asked.

"Yes," Aunt Bess said. "Swept her right away from much younger men during her first season. She is extraordinarily beautiful. She made quite a splash that year. The Dalrymples thought it a good match, despite a rather marked age difference. Poindexter's is a well-respected title, you know."

"She married an old man?" Repugnance sounded in Emily's voice. "*I* certainly would not want to marry an old man, no matter how exalted the title."

"Just as well, Em," her brother said. "None of your suitors at the moment even boasts a title."

Emily's response to this comment was an indignant "Hmph."

The carriage soon deposited them at the Meridon door. Going through the receiving line, Sarah observed that Aunt Bess and Lady Dalrymple were delighted to see each other again; that the Lords Dalrymple and Poindexter were clearly bored, casting eyes at the card room now and then; and that Lady Poindexter, tall, blond, and totally self-assured—the reputed beauty of several seasons ago—had lost none of the allure for which she was known.

Emily and Charles were immediately absorbed by a bevy of young people. Sarah and Aunt Bess conversed with certain of the local gentry. Sarah looked around the room discreetly for Matthew and was disappointed to find he had not yet arrived.

# Seven

Owing to a minor mishap with a carriage wheel, the group from Markholme arrived late. Looking around the room for Sarah, Matthew finally spotted her dancing with a man near his own age. He smothered a twinge of jealousy. Then another couple on the floor caught his attention—that is, the woman did—Annalisa. He drew in his breath and steeled himself for the expected pain. Strangely, it did not come. Muted regret, nostalgia, but no pain.

As the dance ended, Sarah's partner returned her to her aunt on the other side of the room. Matthew had barely taken a step to go to Sarah when Annalisa intercepted him.

"Ah, Matthew—Lord Markholme—how absolutely divine to see you again. Though I should scold you, I think, for ignoring poor little me when you were in town earlier."

She looked coy in emphasizing his title. Her long, silver-blond hair was swept up in a sophisticated style that admirably suited her delicate features. Emerald green eyes, a creamy complexion, and an excellent figure delineated her beauty. Wearing a white gown with a silver overskirt and a not-quite-scandalously-low neckline, she was, indeed, a vision to behold. She also seemed well aware of her effect on any male over the age of ten.

"Lady Poindexter." He bowed low over her hand, then raised his eyes coolly to hers. "I trust you are enjoying the evening. Lady Meridon seems to have achieved quite a crush."

What *did* one say to a woman with whom one had been passionately in love? Oh, glad you noticed me? Does a title make me acceptable now? Her perfume, heady and exotic, had wafted through his dreams for years. It now touched a familiar chord to which his body responded despite the cynicism of his thought. Her hand on his arm prevented him from walking toward Sarah.

Her voice was low and seductive. "I had hoped to see you before this. But never mind, I counted on your being here and I have saved you a dance—you see? A waltz. I am so sorry I promised the supper dance to Nathan Bartholomew now that you are here."

She pouted prettily and held out her card. With others looking on, he had little choice but to sign.

"Oh, is it not just wonderful to have his lordship back with us after all this time?" Annalisa had not removed her hand from his arm as she addressed the others nearby. There was a disconcerting brightness to her eyes. As she was claimed by her next dance partner, she turned so that her breast grazed Matthew's arm.

He raised an eyebrow at Adrian and, looking over Adrian's shoulder, saw that Sarah had observed at least part of what had just transpired.

"Old embers still burning?" Adrian asked in an aside. Matthew shrugged almost imperceptibly and moved toward Sarah to claim her for the dance just starting.

The intricate steps of the dance made conversation difficult, but he managed to explain their late arrival.

"Did you miss me?" he asked lightly.

"Of course," she responded in the same vein.

As the dance ended he walked her back to her place, conscious of the warmth of her hand on his arm. They chatted about inconsequential matters as he sat out the next dance with her and Aunt Bess. He started to write his name in her dance card.

"It would not do for us to engage in more than two dances," Sarah warned, "lest we start the gossips buzzing."

"You have not yet promised the supper dance?"

"No. I hoped to share it with you."

"Good."

Her lack of coyness pleased him. They were both engaged with others for the next dances. When they met in the dance patterns, she had a ready smile for him.

He also occasionally met Annalisa on the dance floor. She repeatedly tried to catch his eye as her partners twirled her through the sets. Her attempts to attract his attention were subtle enough, but they did not go unnoticed by the gossiping chaperones along the wall.

Sitting with Aunt Bess at one point, Sarah observed the blond beauty's interest in Matthew. She scarcely noticed Lady Meridon join the group on the other side of Aunt Bess.

"Well," Lady Meridon announced in her customary demand to be noticed, "I see Annalisa has not lost her touch. 'Twould be no surprise to me if she managed to add Markholme to her court. After all, they were quite the thing during her season—until Poindexter and his thousands per annum came along."

"Markholme does not seem to be succumbing to her lures," another lady said.

"Oh, but he will. Never fear. He will," Lady Meridon insisted knowingly. "No man is ever able to withstand her charms if she chooses to exert them."

Aunt Bess patted Sarah's hand when the conversation on the other side drifted on to something else. "Do not allow that loose tongue to spoil your evening, child. She did not know what she was saying."

"Perhaps she did, though," Sarah said. "After all, she is of the same family. . . . In any event, Matthew is a grown man. He has not lived in a cocoon all these years."

But some of the warmth and gaiety of the evening had disappeared.

The supper dance was the first of two waltzes on the program. Matthew's hand at her waist and hers on his shoulder spread warmth throughout her body. She caught the spicy aroma of his shaving soap and a faint, harder-to-define scent that was his alone.

He guided her expertly and gracefully. He had to bend slightly to accommodate his body to her shorter stance, but they moved together with graceful artistry. Moreover, they seemed to be enjoying each other, as she smiled up at him and he gazed laughingly into her eyes.

"We fit together well here, do we not?" he asked.

"It would seem so. At least we have managed to stay off each other's toes."

He drew her slightly closer and whispered, "Do you think we will fit together equally well elsewhere?"

She blushed rosily. "Are you trying to discompose me, sir?"

"Only a little. But you did not miss a step, did you?" He chuckled and swung her around in a great circle.

Matthew's impulse was to pull her even closer, but a public display would set the tabbies to buzzing. Besides, he had no idea how she would react. Having her so close, but not close enough was exquisitely tantalizing. Never had he felt this way in merely dancing with another woman. Nor had he ever been quite so overly protective of a woman's reputation before.

Finally, and much too soon, the dance ended and the participants traipsed into the supper room. On the way, Matthew leaned down to speak softly to Sarah.

"I enjoyed that waltz immensely," he said. "Next time, we shall not be limited to just two dances, shall we?"

She laughed. "If it occurs after we are wed, we should raise just as many eyebrows by dancing together at all. Married folk are not expected to be in each other's pockets all the time, you know."

"Perhaps we will set a new trend."

Matthew led Sarah to a table with the Marquis of Trenville and his partner, Sybil Meridon. The group also included Emily and Hendley and another couple. Conversation flowed easily, but neither Matthew nor Sarah took much of a role in it.

In his arms, Sarah had been unable to comprehend anything save his presence—the strength and grace of his body and the warmth reflected in his gray eyes. Now, she tried to record each nuance of feeling to be examined later. Lady Meridon's unfortunate remarks came back to her. Do exercise some restraint, she told herself. There is no need to make a cake of yourself over a man enamored of another woman.

Matthew, too, admonished himself to control his emotions. It was one thing to be polite and decorous toward a future wife in a contractual marriage. It was quite another to be preoccupied by romantic aspects of her person. Had he not been down that road before with disastrous result? Never again would he be undone by his feelings for a woman.

And there—just across the room—was the woman who had occasioned that disaster. He recalled vividly his sense of betrayal, his utter despair, on hearing the lovely Annalisa—his Annalisa—would marry the titled, wealthy, and politically powerful Lord Poindexter. When Matthew confronted her, she pledged undying love for him and suggested they run away together. In the end, though, she married the older man, sending Matthew a note saying she had to do this for her family. And, God help him, he believed her, seeing his unattainable lover as a martyr to a noble cause. Years later, he realized what others had seen all along: the lady herself required title, wealth, and an elevated position in society—none of which a low-ranking young officer could provide.

He had viewed Poindexter with a curious blend of pity, contempt, and envy. The man had captured a young beauty, but his possessions, not his person, had won her. Now the fates, with their great taste for irony, turned those youthful emotions—the contempt, at least—on himself, for now, he, too, had been selected as a marriage partner merely for material gain. True, he and Sarah gained equally, but how did that lessen the stark reality of the situation?

Suddenly Emily's voice intruded on his musings.

"Why should it matter who one's partner is?" she said to Sybil. "Charles is quite the best dance partner I have ever had and we intend to do the next waltz together, no matter what the tabbies have to say of it."

"That says little for the rest of us who have partnered you," Hendley said dryly.

"Oh. I did not mean to slight anyone." Her glance swept the men at the table, each of whom had taken the floor with her earlier. "It is just that Charles and I have practiced and practiced together . . ."

"Bravo, Emily," Matthew said. "What a silly notion—to give up a perfectly good dance partner just because you are related to him." He looked at Sarah pointedly.

With a sigh of resignation that was pure sham, she handed over her dance card for him to put his name next to another country dance later in the evening.

When it came time for the waltz with Annalisa, she floated into his arms and, for a split second, as her perfume assailed his senses, he was carried back to being a young lieutenant violently in love with the season's reigning debutante.

"Oh, do they not make a most striking couple now?" Lady Meridon's voice carried beyond her immediate listeners.

Sarah, dancing with Trenville, had to admit Matthew and his partner were indeed a picture to behold. But the admission cost her wrenching pain near her heart.

"Beauty is as beauty does," Trenville whispered, squeezing her hand sympathetically. She flashed him a grateful smile.

Tall and elegant, Annalisa was only three inches shorter than Matthew. Her blond beauty provided a stunning complement to his darker good looks. Her white and silver dress in contrast to his formal black attire further enhanced the picture. Annalisa seemed aware of and pleased with the image they presented, almost as if she had orchestrated this scene herself.

She moved closer to him than strict decorum or the

patterns of the dance called for and smiled triumphantly when his hold on her hand tightened.

"Ah, Matthew, how I have missed you," she murmured.

"Ten years later. Surely your husband keeps you from dwelling on the past." His tone was lightly ironic.

She gave a ladylike sniff. "My *husband* is far more interested in his precious horses than in his marriage. Ours is a thoroughly modern marriage. He has his heir and now does just as he pleases. As do I. We are quite comfortable, so long as neither of us makes an untoward spectacle of ourselves or causes tongues wagging too much—and we have not yet done so." She laughed softly.

"So—you find yourself in the enviable position of being able to eat your cake and have it, too."

"Yesss," she trilled. "I have, as you well know, always been one to get what I want." Her look made no secret of exactly what it was she wanted now. "Oh, Matthew, I know you feel that I treated you abominably, but it really could not be helped. The situation was impossible as you know." Her voice was coaxing now. "But I never forgot you, your touch, your kiss . . ." Her voice trailed off to a husky whisper on the last words.

"You appear to have managed well with your life." By seeming to concentrate on the dance patterns, he avoided reacting to her obvious invitation. His own response confused him. He had dreamed of this for years—this woman in his arms, willing and responsive. But now reality was strangely flat. Something was missing.

"Appearances can be deceiving, dear man. Sometimes we find that what seemed absolutely necessary at a given time in our lives is not enough at another." She sounded self-pitying.

As the dance was drawing to a close, she said, "I simply must see you again. Please ride with me tomorrow morning. No one else in this household will stir much before mid-afternoon."

Cursing himself for a fool even as he did so, he agreed to meet her.

# Eight

"So, are you meeting her tomorrow?" Adrian and Matthew were back in the Markholme library having a brandy before retiring, Hendley having already gone up.

"I said I would. I can hardly do otherwise now."

"I know you once had noble and tender feelings for the lady . . . perhaps then she deserved them. But that is no longer true. And you have much more at risk now."

"I know that." Matthew's tone was impatient. "But precisely because of what she once was—what we were to each other—I could not refuse her request to meet."

"Every young buck in London was at least half in love with her in her first season. The rest of us were put off when you managed to cut us out." Adrian chuckled.

"Hah! The joke was on all of us when she married Poindexter."

"Ah, yes, the beautiful Miss Dalrymple gained herself a title. Her place in society is secure. And—she has a wealthy husband who allows her free rein."

"So much for thinking mutual affection should count for anything," Matthew said bitterly. "God! What a fool I was!"

"No one but you faults you for your feelings. She was—and is—a damned attractive woman. Still rather charming, too, though a mite predatory. Do take care, my friend."

"I appreciate your concern, Adrian, but I am not the ignorant youth I was ten years ago. I am well aware of the capacity for deceit in women. However, she is, as you say, still a powerfully attractive female. I admit to a certain curiosity . . . and probably a degree of egotism."

"You seem to lump all women together."

"Well, why not? Other than your mother or sisters, how many have you found to be honest and forthright in their dealings with you?"

"Not many. However, there are few men I trust as I do you, either. But your Sarah may be just such a woman."

"*My* Sarah? Sarah is very much her own person. But I hope you are right about her. Time will tell."

"And I sincerely hope you are not deceiving yourself about her—or the Lady Annalisa. Well . . . forewarned is forearmed. I have said all I will say. But of course, I shall be available to pick up the pieces again if necessary." Adrian saluted with his glass.


The next morning Annalisa was already at the appointed place when Matthew arrived on his big bay stallion. Lady Poindexter was properly accompanied by a groom—one had to keep up appearances, Matthew thought cynically—but the servant had clearly been instructed to keep his distance. At her suggestion, she and Matthew both dismounted and walked slowly along the edge of a fallow field.

"Your return to society is a welcome one, my lord." She peeped at him from beneath the brim of a dark green hat that matched her fashionable riding habit. A perky green feather reflected her own flirtatious manner.

"A reluctant one. I am not giving up a style of living and a career I have loved without mixed feelings."

"I suppose our parting was a happy circumstance for you then, for I am sure I would have been most unacceptable as a follower of the drum."

"Besotted as I was," he said, "I could not have agreed then to that assessment. After all, scores of other officers' wives manage very well. You probably could have done so, too."

She looked as though she did not know whether to be pleased at his admission to having been "besotted" or chagrined by his rather dismissive tone.

"I would hardly have been the wife of a high-ranking officer. Even with a modest marriage portion, we would have lived on a decidedly lower scale than I could have accepted. Not to mention missing London society. In the end, we would have hated each other, my dear."

"Perhaps. But the past is past, eh?"

"Truly. But that need not mean the present and future have no promise for us, surely? Now that you apparently intend to secure a place in society, why should we not continue our—umm—friendship?"

"Do you ignore the fact that you are married? Or that I may one day marry as well?"

"Of what consequence is that in our circles? Marital fidelity is not exactly the expected thing, you know."

Surprised—though her conversation the previous evening should have prepared him for this encounter—Matthew stopped and faced her directly. Looping his reins over his arm, he took both her hands in his.

"I am flattered, Annalisa," he said gently, "but I will not be any woman's cicisbeo. And a conventional sense of honor does not allow me to deliberately cuckold another man—no matter how strongly I might be tempted." And, truth to tell, I am not even tempted now, he thought with amazement.

"I fail to see how *honor* fits into this discussion," Annalisa said sharply. "I indicated to you the nature of my marriage. Poindexter and I understand each other."

"Yes, he does seem to be a very understanding man."

"Perhaps your affections are engaged by that Longbourne chit," Annalisa said sarcastically. "Or is it her reputed fortune that is so attractive?"

"Miss Longbourne has no place in this discussion."

Matthew's voice took on a flinty quality totally alien to

the young lieutenant she had once handled so easily, but a quality not lost on any soldier in the major's command. Nor was it lost on Annalisa. She abruptly switched tactics. She squeezed his hands and looked at him with a slight pout on her well-shaped lips.

"Are you saying you no longer care for me? You seemed happy enough to see me yesterday evening."

"Of course I was pleased to see you," he said politely. "You are a beautiful woman and were always an interesting companion. As a much younger man, I was devastated to think that my regard carried so little weight with you." She started to smile triumphantly and leaned toward him, when he continued, "But time heals all wounds."

Her face flushed with anger and her eyes became as hard as the stone they so resembled. Jerking her hands from his grip, she nearly spat her next words.

"The circumstances of your gaining your title, my lord, are well-known to the *ton* and, quite frankly, it would appear that your situation will be in most particulars similar to my own. In a few months' time you may sing a different tune."

She coldly allowed him to assist her in remounting. Largely for the benefit of her groom, she said, "Perhaps we will meet at the Pilkington soirees later in the week."

Amazingly, her ill feeling did not disturb him overmuch. Once, he thought as he rode slowly home, I would have run after her all apologetic, ready to swear to anything she desired. Now, it was not emerald eyes hard with anger that occupied his thoughts, but violet eyes sparkling with laughter.

However, Annalisa's last angry retort disturbed him. *Were* his circumstances the same as hers? Was his marrying for wealth to secure an inheritance any less reprehensible than her doing so to gain a title and social standing?

Sarah spent the night tossing and turning, reliving her moments in Matthew's arms, recalling his words and expressions. She knew her neighbors noted the new Lord Markholme wasted little time in laying claim to the elusive Miss Longbourne. She felt most of them approved, with Lady Meridon, of course, a possible exception.

Their third dance raised eyebrows. It was a lively country dance allowing the partners periods of pause while other couples executed steps. The exuberant energy of the steps and public intimacy of the pauses added excitement. And, no, she had not imagined Matthew's reluctance to let her hand go each time they touched. That dance had done much to raise her spirits, coming as it did after his waltz with Lady Poindexter.

Luckily, some of the attention centered then on Markholme and his partner had been deflected. Charles and Emily had put on a spectacular display, such as must have been intended by the originators of the graceful waltz. The onlookers had even forgiven their being brother and sister.

Her own attention had not been so diverted. Clearly there had once been something profound between Matthew and Lady Poindexter. And, just as clearly, the lady was trying to rekindle what had once been there. Sarah recalled his promise never to knowingly embarrass his wife. That he would keep up appearances should be of some comfort, she thought, but it is not.

I want more.

Immediately, Practicality intruded: you cannot logically expect more. You have what you wanted from this alliance—and a handsome, personable, considerate man as a life-partner as well. What more could you demand?

Love.

There. She had actually verbalized it, if only to herself. Love.

Ah, but surely not under these circumstances, Practicality insisted. Be content with what you have. Besides, what business have you of wanting from another—and a virtual stranger at that—what you are unwilling to give?

The weather took a turn for the worse, threatening snow and actually offering intermittent rainstorms. Deep ruts and rivers of mud made travel extremely difficult. Trenville was forced to postpone his departure, though Matthew's sister and her family arrived late one afternoon.

Matthew welcomed them heartily. He and his sister Catherine had always been extraordinarily close. Even the separation caused by his military career had not weakened the tie maintained by letters and short visits.

Catherine's husband, Edward Brockton, a fellow student at Oxford, had lost his heart immediately on meeting his school chum's younger sister, then a girl of fifteen. By the end of her only season in London some three years later, Catherine had turned down two very eligible offers and finally convinced the earnest young churchman that he could be a winner if only he would enter the race.

Eight years had passed. Edward still seemed to think he had won the greatest of prizes and Catherine seemed equally happy, if a bit tired at the moment. Indeed, Catherine and Edward were exhausted, though the two children were as energetic as ever a boy of five and a girl of three could be. They were unpracticed, but adorable in making their bow and curtsy to this uncle neither of them could remember.

The following morning, rested and refreshed, Catherine was the first of the Brocktons to enter the breakfast room. Matthew sat reading a three-day old newspaper as he finished his meal.

"Are we the early birds?" She greeted him with a kiss on his cheek.

"Adrian just left to check on the roads. He is anxious to make it to Wiltshire for Christmas. Hendley usually comes down somewhat later."

"Good. I have you all to myself."

"I'm all yours. Just don't start ripping up at me as you were wont to do in days of yore."

"As I remember, you, more often than not, were the one doing the ripping. I never quite understood why you did not like having a little girl tagging after you all the time. Already, I see my son having the same problem," she said, laughing.

"Soon enough, he will not mind at all having a female tagging after him."

"Let us not rush that, though. Now. Tell me about Miss Longbourne."

"I wrote you the particulars—she is mistress of the neighboring estate. You know the terms of both her inheritance and mine. Bit of a muddle, what with her once having been betrothed, albeit unofficially, to Cousin Robert. But the situation is sorting itself out."

"Was her mother not the one who . . ."

"Yes. Sarah is the daughter of the woman who jilted Uncle Matt. Ironic, eh?"

"What is she like? One of our neighbors told me she is a bluestocking. Is she truly an antidote?"

"No. Not at all. She has quite a lively wit and is every bit as stubborn and opinionated as you, dear sister mine. Seems my fate to go through life fighting off strong-minded females." He grinned at her.

"Oh, dear. Is she one of those domineering sorts that manage everyone else's life? I mean, she *will* be the countess and I should hate to think she will always be wanting to tell the vicar and his wife how to go on."

"You needn't fear Sarah will try to control your lives. You will find her very supportive. I feel certain the two of you will get on well together."

"Will the two of *you* get on well together?" Her gray eyes, so like her brother's, were warmly sympathetic. "I must say, I had hoped for a different sort of alliance for you, Matthew. I would have you find the same sort of happiness I have with Edward."

"There is much to be said for a marriage that brings social and material advantage not only to the immediate parties, but to their families as well." As he listened to his own words, Annalisa's parting comment sprang to mind.

"There are benefits to all of us," Catherine said, "but you must know that neither Edward nor I would welcome material improvements in our lives at your expense. Marriage can be difficult under the best of conditions and love helps tremendously in smoothing out the rough spots."

"Love." He tried to keep the bitterness out of his voice. "Love is different things for different people. My venture in that direction was an impossible journey into a swampy jungle of despair and disappointment. Never again!"

"Oh, Matthew."

"Mutual respect and tolerance cannot be too disastrous as a foundation for marriage."

"But it takes love, too," she insisted.

"You do know, do you not, that you and Edward are rare exceptions to the rule when it comes to marriages?"

"Not so very rare."

"You must agree that few marriages have fairy-tale outcomes." Again he recalled Annalisa discussing her "understanding" with her apparently indifferent husband.

"True. But fairy-tale endings are possible—they just take a great deal of work."

"This is not a fairy tale," he said firmly. "It is an alliance designed to save the title and property of this earldom and allow my bride to retain rights to her inheritance. Both Sarah and I have fully accepted that premise for our relationship."

"Oh, Matthew, it sounds so dull!"

"I seriously doubt life with Sarah will ever be dull." Maddening at times, but never dull.

"Is she pretty?"

"Hmmm. Is she pretty? Yes, I suppose she is." He noted her eyebrows lift in surprise that he was unable to answer such a simple question about his betrothed. "You can judge for yourself this afternoon," he said with a trace of impatience. "She will call upon you then. I sent word this morning of your arrival."

# Nine

As Matthew and his guests welcomed the three Long-bournes and Mrs. Carstairs, Sarah felt discreet, but intense scrutiny from Matthew's sister.

Sarah scored an immediate hit with the Brocktons when she expressed interest in meeting their children. With curly dark hair and their father's warm brown eyes, both exhibited the ready curiosity of children who know themselves to be cherished.

Aside from a fleeting reference to the need for an heir, Matthew and Sarah had not discussed children. He was pleased to see the ease with which she handled his niece and nephew. As she knelt to speak directly to the children and indirectly to their parents of attractions in their new home, Matthew caught her eye and smiled to see her blush. Once again their thoughts had been traveling the same path.

When the children had been sent back to the temporary nursery, Catherine turned to Sarah.

"Edward and I are very happy to be removing to Derbyshire, Miss Longbourne, and we want to thank you, as well as Matthew, for making this possible." Her husband nodded his concurrence.

"Oh, please. We must use our Christian names." Sarah leaned from her chair to touch Catherine's hand. "After all, we shall be family soon and I hope we will become friends as well. Since the Dentons' eldest daughter wed

Lord Benson, I have been quite without a close female friend. I hope you will fill that void."

"I should like that very much," Catherine said simply.

"If the weather permits tomorrow, perhaps you will allow me to show you the vicarage," Sarah said. "You will find it quite spacious—one of the previous pastors had nine children!"

"Having space will be a welcome change," Catherine replied. "My gracious, there is so much happening between now and the new year!"

"Yes," Sarah said, "and the season in London to follow. I do hope you will be able to accompany us."

"I understand you are sponsoring your sister this season." Catherine glanced across the room to where Emily chatted with her brother and Hendley. "I made my comeout from Markholme House. Such a pleasant time for a young girl."

"Until I swept you away from all that," Edward said with a smile.

"As I recall, I had the devil's own time bringing you up to scratch. But in the end, perseverance won out." Catherine smiled fondly at her husband, her gray eyes twinkling. For an instant, the two of them shut themselves away from the others. Sarah wondered if she and Matthew would ever be so tuned to each other.

The next day produced better weather. Trenville departed for Christmas with his family, promising to return for the wedding. The excursion to the vicarage took place as planned and the Brocktons were delighted with their new home.

The thirty people invited to the dinner party at Markholme included all of those who had attended the Rosemont party earlier and many who had attended Lady Meridon's ball. Separately, both Sarah and Matthew would have omitted the Meridon group, but despite Lady Meridon's being a gossipy know-all, she was not deliberately malicious and did not deserve such a cut direct—however annoying or disconcerting the presence of her niece might be.

Meanwhile, Matthew discussed details of restoring ten-ant farms to their productive best with Edward, whose in-come came in part from certain local farms. Edward was startled when Sarah joined these discussions. When it dawned on him that Matthew apparently intended to leave her in charge of overseeing the entire earldom in his ab-sence, Brockton was astonished.

"You cannot mean to leave a woman in charge of all this," he said with a sweeping gesture as he and Matthew sat over their port one evening.

"I admit to reservations, but I agreed to allow Sarah to handle it. She is very determined and seems to know what she is talking about. Howard is reliable, too."

"Still, this a huge undertaking for a man, let alone a woman. I confess I would find it intimidating."

"As do I. But then your expertise is theology and mine is the army. . . . Sarah truly believes she can do the job."

"And you are willing to let her? Are you not afraid that you may end with the estate in as much or more of a mud-dle as you found it?"

"There is that possibility, I suppose. But since the blunt to make all these improvements comes with her, I would feel a real blighter should I refuse her."

"I understand, but I wonder that you are willing to take such a risk. Once you are married, you will control her property and wealth—indeed, you will control *her*. Legally, you will have authority to do whatever you wish."

"True." Matthew gave his brother-in-law a meaningful look. "But I gave her my word and that's that. I trust you will support her in any way you can."

"Of course."

Sarah, anxious about the announcement to be made at the party at Markholme Hall, chose to wear a finely woven blue woolen gown. It was trimmed with antique lace at the edges of sleeves that ended in a flare just below the elbow. A wide neckline, straight from the shoulders, curved into a soft "V" over the beginning swell of her breasts. With small sapphire earrings, she wore a necklace of sapphires from which dangled a larger stone just at the hint of her cleavage. There was also a ring. Matthew had presented the jewelry to her earlier in the day.

He arrived unexpectedly in mid-afternoon and asked to see her privately.

"Catherine said you should have these before this evening." He opened the case to show her the jewels. "They have been in the family since the time of Charles II." He set the case on a table and took her hand in his to place the ring on her finger.

"How beautiful." Sarah admired the ring, an oval sapphire encircled by diamonds.

She lifted her head and caught her breath. Violet eyes locked with gray ones. A thrill whirled through her as she felt his nearness and the firm clasp of his hand. He released her hand, slipped his arms around her, and drew her against him, lowering his lips to hers. Powerless to resist, she responded as eagerly as she had the first time he kissed her.

"Sarah, I have wanted to do this again for days." He planted soft little kisses from the lobe of her ear to the sensitive joining of her neck and shoulder. Whatever she might have replied was lost as his lips again claimed hers. Finally, both seemed to regain their senses and drew slightly apart.

"Did Catherine say this is the way Cameron men always present their betrothal ring?" Her breathing was uneven.

"No. This was entirely my own idea." He sought her lips again.

"Mmm." The muffled sound might have been anything, but her response as she leaned into his body was enthusiastic.

"And a good idea it was, if I do say so." He took a step back and grinned at her.

"I don't know what came over me." She was blushing furiously.

"I do," he said wickedly.

"What you must think . . ."

"I think, Miss Longbourne, that we will suit quite well in this respect." He laughed softly and tried to pull her back into his arms, but she stepped away and put up her hands in mild protest.

"No more. We mustn't, you know."

"No, I do not know, but I shall abide by your wishes." She giggled at his expression. He resembled nothing so much as a little boy told to wait until dinner for another sweet.

"I love the ring." She politely ushered him out.

"Until tonight," he said at the door. He bent quickly to catch her by surprise with a quick kiss and left.

She stood a moment, amazed. Never had she been kissed so thoroughly. She was again shocked at her own lack of control, but he seemed as caught up as she. Perhaps we will "suit quite well in this respect" she mused. But will that be enough? There had been no tender words of love.

Well, she upbraided herself, what did you expect?

Equally overwhelmed, Matthew questioned his own behavior. He had intended no more than a chaste little peck. Carried away again, eh, Cameron? Again, she had responded with warmth and passion. Just how experienced was his prospective wife? She was beyond the age of most women on the marriage mart and she admitted to more than passing knowledge of—how had she put it?—"the mating process and procreation." Had she and Robert indulged themselves before that tragic accident?

With this thought came a flash of anger, much of it directed at himself. He had once agonized over the thought of Annalisa in the arms of another, but never since had he resented any woman's possible affection for another. And in this instance, the competition was a dead man against whom he was powerless. Anyway, why in thunder should he care so much? This marriage was basically a business arrangement. If they both enjoyed a bit of passion as an added benefit of the arrangement, all the better.

Nevertheless, by the time he arrived at his own stable, he had worked himself into a "right proper tear" as one of the grooms later reported.

The Rosemont folk arrived early to help introduce the earl's family to their new neighbors. Matthew, impeccable in black evening attire, greeted them formally, bowing over the hands of the ladies. Sarah attributed his reserve to nervousness about the announcement to be made later.

Polite confusion reigned as new guests arrived. Matthew anticipated the arrival of Lady Meridon's group uneasily, for it would, of course, include the earl Poindexter and his wife. At the Pilkington soirees, Annalisa had adopted a cool, polite demeanor even when Matthew stood up with her for a country dance.

Tonight, the Meridon party were the last to arrive and Annalisa was effusively apologetic, charming, and apparently determined to ignore previous unpleasantness. In a light green silk gown with a sheer overskirt of darker fabric and dangerously low neckline, Annalisa instantly became the center of attention. She wore a fortune in emeralds that not only complemented her green and silver beauty, but provided ample evidence that Annalisa Dalrymple's choice of the aging Lord Poindexter had been generously rewarded.

As the guests divided into various conversational groups, Annalisa seized an opportunity to speak to her host.

"Will you be removing to the city for the season?" She spoke softly so that he had to lean nearer to hear her.

"Yes. Hendley and I are awaiting orders from the foreign office." He would have moved away, but she put her hand on his arm and smiled at him intimately. He knew—and he assumed she knew, too—that this little tableau was not lost on others.

"Surely we may have some time together before you answer duty's call again," she said in the same intimate voice. "It will be much easier for us to arrange to meet in the city. Here in the country everyone is so much in each other's pockets."

"Annalisa . . ." he started, in a firm tone, but then his sister was at his elbow.

"Do pardon me," Catherine said sweetly, "but I must have a word with Matthew."

Murmuring an apology, Matthew went with his sister, both seemingly unaware that Lady Poindexter was left fuming.

"I thought you needed rescuing," Catherine said.

"I did."

"That little *tête-à-tête* was not exactly the thing on this night, do you think?" Her disapproval was plain.

Lady Meridon raised her eyebrows at her niece when Matthew escorted Sarah in to dinner and seated her at his right. His sister graced the other end of the table. Annalisa was placed halfway down the table from Sarah. The meal had been prepared with skill and elegantly served. Conversation flowed quietly and properly on either side of the table.

"For one long away from society, my lord," Sarah quietly teased, "you handle this affair extraordinarily well."

"Thank you, my dear." His voice dropped to a near whisper. "It helps to have a sister—not to mention a fiancée—who never left those exalted ranks." He smiled to see her blush.

When the desserts had been served and the table cleared, Matthew signaled for flutes of champagne.

"My friends." He rose and lifted his glass. "I thank you for welcoming my family and me. The more we get to know this area and its people, the happier we are to be here."

There were murmurs of "Hear, hear" as guests raised their glasses, but waited for Matthew to continue. He clasped Sarah's elbow and drew her to her feet beside him.

"I should also like to announce that Miss Sarah Longbourne has increased my happiness a thousandfold by agreeing to marry me. Will you join me in a toast to my future wife?"

A few gasps—Lady Meridon's in particular—greeted his

announcement. Gazing down both sides of the table, Matthew saw only general approval and smiles of congratulation. Until his glance fell on Annalisa Poindexter. Anger and contempt slithered across her beautifully sculpted features before she hid them behind a bland mask. She raised her glass at his toast, but he noticed she did not drink.

Attention focused on Sarah as the ladies withdrew to the drawing room. Lady Poindexter was unusually quiet until the gentlemen rejoined them. Then she brightened and flirted outrageously with any male near her. Her husband looked on indifferently. Matthew had taken a position near Sarah's chair when Annalisa approached to make a small production of wishing them joy.

"My lord," she said, ensuring that most of the room was attending, "I congratulate you on a most advantageous match. I am sure Miss Longbourne will bring you much in the way of . . . happiness." Lady Poindexter was not so vulgar as to mention outright the material side of the marriage, but her intent was clear.

Sensing Sarah stiffen, Matthew placed his hand on her shoulder and gave it a gentle squeeze. "Thank you, my lady," he said coolly. "We expect to bring each other much in the way of happiness." He deliberately used her own phrasing.

"Your good wishes are most . . . gratifying." Employing the same sort of pause Lady Poindexter had used, Sarah smiled up at Matthew. The look of understanding that passed between them was not lost on Annalisa.

# Ten

Afterward, Sarah recalled the next weeks as a haze of frenzied activity, including fittings for new gowns, meetings on estate matters, and plans to remove to the city soon after the new year. Details of the wedding and Christmas festivities required careful planning.

Matthew and Sarah saw little of each other in these weeks, except at social events they both felt obligated to attend. Even when he might have spent a quiet evening in his own library, he exerted himself to make a showing at these affairs because eventually he expected to take his seat in the House of Lords to represent these people and their interests.

A community Christmas Ball highlighted the area's seasonal festivities. Sarah always enjoyed this annual event that brought together people of all classes. It had the atmosphere of a country fair and those attending expected to have a good time without regard to trying to impress their neighbors. Servants and farmers from various estates looked forward to the opportunity to catch up on their friends' doings. Many a new romance began at the Axton Christmas Ball.

The news of their impending marriage having swept the district, Sarah and Matthew were the star attraction this year. Matthew was pleased by the regard and genuine affection people accorded his prospective bride. As one grizzled old farmer said to him, "You be gettin' a mighty fine woman, my lord. Mighty fine."

People withheld judgment on the new earl, though they were inclined to greet him warmly. Cautious optimism and hope—long absent as the ongoing war with Napoleon's forces drained the country's resources—now brightened the outlook.

"You know, Richard," Matthew said to Hendley, "here—this—is why we were mucking around in the mud and enduring the heat and dust in the Peninsula. Sometimes, we soldiers lose sight of why we do what we do."

"Yes, sir. And we also do it for *that.*" With a twinkle in his eyes, Hendley nodded toward the entrance as Sarah and Emily reentered the ballroom.

Matthew chuckled. "One cannot argue with that logic."

"Hmmm. Would not have thought logic came into it much." Hendley grinned.

"Hah!" Matthew's tone became serious. "It rarely does—and therein lies a great deal of pain." He tapped his companion's chest with his forefinger. "Have a care, my friend. Have a care."

"No fear of that, sir. I am not in serious danger—yet." The look in Hendley's eyes as he watched Emily dancing with a local swain belied his light, bantering tone.

The Poindexter-Dalrymple party were to be at the Meridon estate through the Christmas season, so they, too, appeared at the village Christmas Ball. The gentlemen of that party were amiable enough, but the ladies generally held themselves aloof. Seeing Sarah take the floor with "Little" Joe Johnson, son of a tenant farmer, Annalisa found a position near Matthew.

"I wonder that you condone your future countess's choice of dancing partner, my lord." She barely controlled the sneer in her voice.

"I believe it was he who asked her to dance," Matthew replied. "He is not making a spectacle of them, so how could I possibly disapprove? We have both observed less decorous behavior at Almack's, I am sure."

"Miss Longbourne is inordinately familiar with the locals, is she not? I should think that would be of some concern to you when your army duties take you away."

"I cannot conceive why," Matthew said coolly, ignoring the innuendo. "Would you care to dance?" he asked to forestall this line of discussion and was immediately sorry when he realized the musicians had struck up a waltz.

"I would love to," she purred and glided into his arms.

The waltz, a new dance, was considered slightly scandalous—if not wholly so in some circles. The gentry had the floor more or less to themselves as they performed for the rest of the ballroom. Several couples whirled and glided to the music. Matthew noticed that Sarah had taken the floor with his brother-in-law and Catherine was dancing with Charles.

He was uncomfortably conscious of the fact that—just as they had at the Meridon ball—he and Annalisa commanded an inordinate amount of attention. He was also keenly aware of the attractions of the woman in his arms. Her exotic perfume worked its magic to stimulate memories of long forgotten desires. Annalisa sensed her effect on him.

"Ah hah! You have missed me, have you not?" she cooed.

"One does not forget easily the first woman he ever fancied himself in love with," Matthew admitted.

"Only fancied?"

"In retrospect, that seems to be the case."

"Oh, Matthew." She pushed closer to him. "You know you want me as much as I want you."

"That is not exactly the point, is it?" He deliberately allowed more space between their bodies.

"Perhaps not. But it is the truth. Do you deny it?"

"I do not deny that you are an attractive woman," he responded diplomatically.

"I suppose the real point, then, is your sadly misplaced sense of honor," she said petulantly. "Surely, you are not

pretending that your proposed marriage will be anything
but a marriage of convenience?"

"The circumstances of my marriage need concern only
my bride and me," he said stiffly.

"But the circumstances of your marriage are generally
known, my lord."

"No. However much vulgar conjecture there may be on
the subject, they are not, my lady, 'generally known.' " His
voice had a hard edge.

"Have it your way, Matthew. I am sure Miss Longbourne
is aware of the realities of our kinds of marriage as is Poindexter. No one would expect us to forego a chance at happiness. It requires only discretion."

He could not come up with a reply that would not be a
lie or an insult. Obviously she assumed his marriage would
be as cold and impersonal as hers apparently was. That was
not what he had visualized. But what *had* he visualized?

One of her barbs took hold. Many a soldier in the field
discovered his wife had taken a lover in his absence. Would
Major Cameron fall victim to that kind of pain? He
doubted Sarah would lower herself to such behavior—but
was that because he desperately *wanted* to believe in her?
And in his own growing attraction to her?

Annalisa was right—Sarah knew the circumstances of
their marriage, but he was mindful of his promise never
to embarrass her. He admitted to himself, not without a
sense of wonder, that he no longer felt overwhelming desire for Annalisa, but neither could he deny remembered
attraction. Good God! A man would have to be dead not
to be flattered when a beautiful woman practically threw
herself at him.

When the dance ended, he pointedly returned her ladyship to her husband. Coward, he accused himself.

Gazing from across the room, Sarah was furious at seeing Annalisa in Matthew's arms again, but there was nothing in his behavior to criticize. She wondered what they
discussed so earnestly. Not the usual innocuous patter one
engaged in on the dance floor—of that she was sure.

She concentrated on Edward's conversation. As they left the floor, they were joined by Emily and Hendley and the thought flitted across Sarah's mind that her sister was being too marked in her attentions to the young lieutenant. They do make a handsome couple, she thought, but during the season Emily will meet many eligible young men, certainly more eligible than a young soldier with limited prospects.

Christmas passed with the traditional Yule log and caroling. Matthew and Sarah exchanged gifts privately when he visited Rosemont late Christmas day. In a festive red gown, she sat next to him on a settee in the drawing room. He presented her a beautiful hand-carved ivory fan, its outer pieces enamelware with a vine of roses worked into the design. Fully opened, the fan displayed in silhouette a young woman with a parasol strolling in a Chinese garden. It was an exquisite piece of work.

"It is lovely," she said almost reverently. When she looked up at him, he saw tears in her eyes.

She, in turn, gave him a gold watch etched on the front with an elaborate rendition of his initials. Around the edge of the back was a similar design, but in the middle was written "Christmas, 1813." Flipping the watch open, he found on the inside of the lid a miniature of his bride-to-be.

"How on earth did you manage this—complete with a portrait? You did not procure such an elegant gift in Derbyshire."

"I sent the portrait with Adrian and commissioned him with the task. It came on the mail coach two days ago and I could hardly wait to give it to you."

"I have never received a gift I will treasure so much as this one." His voice was husky.

He put his arm around her shoulder and pulled her closer, kissing her tenderly on her temple. But that was not enough for either of them and his lips found hers as her hand crept up to caress his cheek.

His breath uneven, Matthew knew if they did not stop immediately, he would take her right here in the drawing room where anyone might walk in on them. He drew away from her gently.

"A few more days," he whispered.

"Yes." Desire showed in her eyes.

Then she seemed to come to herself and she blushed furiously. Once again she appeared caught off guard by her own passion.

"I am shameless." It was almost a whisper. She put her hand to her mouth, seeming to realize she had spoken aloud.

He chuckled. "I guess we both are." He hugged her briefly. "Thank you for my Christmas gift," he said softly, leaving it intentionally unclear whether he referred only to the watch.

"Thank you, Matthew, for this lovely fan. I hope . . ." She paused, unable to articulate her feelings.

He waited, his eyes gently questioning.

"I hope neither of us is ever sorry about all this."

"Are you having second thoughts?"

"Oh, no!"

"Good. Neither am I." He kissed her on the forehead, not daring to allow himself her lips again.

Five days later they were married.

# Eleven

Edward Brockton officiated at his first marriage ceremony in his new parish. In a silk gown of antique white with satin and lace trim and with a veil of antique Belgian lace, Sarah fairly floated down the aisle on the arm of her brother. Afterward she did not remember getting there on her own. She did remember Matthew's face as her destination and everything seemed all right once he smiled at her.

During the carriage ride back to Rosemont, a weak winter sun did little to alleviate the bitter cold. Sarah snuggled close to Matthew savoring his warmth as he tucked her cloak around her and covered them both with a lap robe.

"Thank goodness we have only two miles to go," he said.

"Yes." Her mind did not deal with distance or even the cold. She felt panicky. What had she done? She did not even know this man and here she was—tied to him for life. She turned to look at him and he read the alarm in her eyes. He slipped his arm around her and drew her close.

"It is somewhat overwhelming, is it not?" He kissed the top of her head. "But I will try to ensure that you are never sorry for having chosen to marry me."

"And I, you." Their eyes held for a moment, then she lowered her gaze. Her moment of panic was gone. They sat in companionable silence the rest of the way.

A wedding breakfast for immediate family and members of the wedding party gave way to a party for additional guests in the drawing room. Champagne and many toasts at both affairs caused Sarah to be thankful for a short winter day and a threatening storm that urged guests to leave early. *I should be sadly tipsy,* she told herself, *if this were a long summer day!*

Darkness was already enveloping the land when Matthew and Sarah set out for the short journey to Markholme. Trenville and Hendley were staying at Rosemont; the Brocktons had long since removed to their own lodgings; and many of the servants had been granted a holiday in honor of the wedding. The newlyweds would have Markholme Hall more or less to themselves.

"The staff have done their best to prepare your suite for you," Matthew said as they climbed the stairs, "but, as you know, there has not been a countess in residence for many years. I am sure you will wish to redecorate. Indeed, you will probably need to redo the whole house."

"Yes." Chatting about the mundane concealed her nervousness. "There is no hurry. We can shop in the city."

Her chamber did show years of neglect and wear, but the servants had done a heroic job of making it clean and welcoming. Twin dressing rooms connected with his chamber. A fire blazed in the fireplace, though its warmth did not reach far.

"Coop will bring supper to my room in a few minutes. I will come for you," he said softly and, with a gentle squeeze of her hand, he exited through the dressing room.

There was a light knock on the hall door and at Sarah's bidding, her own familiar Betsy was there to help her out of the heavy wedding gown she had worn all day. She changed into a delicate nightgown—a flimsy bit of lawn and lace. A matching peignoir fastened with a single ribbon at the low neckline. Sarah smothered a giggle as she donned these garments. Both had seemed so perfect for a bride's wedding night when the set was made up.

"I am going to freeze in this," she said to the maid.

"Mebbe so, my lady, but not for long, I'm thinkin',"

Betsy said pertly. "His lordship will be fair bowled over when he sees you."

"And will that make my freezing worthwhile?"

" 'Tis supposed that it will."

Sarah smiled at the girl's serious tone. Betsy picked up the discarded clothing and quietly left.

A few minutes later, with a soft rap at the dressing room door, Matthew entered, wearing no more than his shirt, open at the neck, breeches, and comfortable slippers. He stared at her a moment.

"You are incredibly lovely, my dear."

"Thank you," she said simply.

"Come." He held the door for her. "Coop has brought us some light refreshment. And I must say my room is warmer than this one."

"Light refreshment?" She surveyed the lavish spread. "How can we justify the effort that went into this feast?"

"We must go through the motions." He grinned and she relaxed a bit. She liked that quirky grin that raised one corner of his mouth higher than the other.

He seated her nearest the fire and sat close to her. They conversed with ease and shared tidbits of food from time to time, but beneath the surface, each nervously anticipated what would come—she with some apprehension, he with eagerness. At last, Matthew rose and extinguished the candles on the table, leaving the room lit now only by a bedside lamp. He extended his hand.

"I have something for you." He nudged her toward his massive bureau on top of which was a small box. He handed it to her. "Open it."

A gold locket and chain rested on a cushion of white velvet. On the front were etched two doves with a twining ribbon and on the back the date. Inside were miniatures of the two of them.

"Emily helped me get your likeness."

"It's lovely." Her eyes sparkled with unshed tears.

"Do you always cry when you receive a gift?" His voice was husky.

"Not always," she murmured.

He took the locket from her and laid it on the dresser. Placing his hands on either side of her face, he settled his mouth on hers. She responded eagerly, her lips parting softly. He slid his hands down her neck and caressed her arms, finally putting his arms around her waist, pulling her to him. Her arms went around his neck and she leaned in to him. Cupping his hands around her, he pulled her even closer. She felt the hard strength of his body.

"We are overdressed." His voice was a husky whisper as he untied the ribbon at her neck and slipped the peignoir and gown off her shoulders to form a pool at her feet. He drew in a shuddering breath as he looked at her. She knew she should feel shy, embarrassed to have a man look at her so boldly, but Matthew's gaze felt warm—and right. Then he removed his shirt, revealing a muscular chest with a "V" of dark hair that disappeared below the waist of his breeches. She noticed a long scar extending diagonally across his chest. She traced it lightly with her fingers. Dropping his shirt, he kicked off his slippers, stripped off his breeches and guided her to the bed.

Sarah had not expected the act of making love with Matthew to be repulsive in any way, but neither did she anticipate such ecstasy. The biggest surprise was the depth and energy of her own response. Matthew patiently brought her to a pitch equal to his own before they achieved together a pinnacle of sensuality she could not possibly have dreamed of before. Yes, there had been a moment of pain, but it was instantly overshadowed by wave after magical wave of pleasure.

Afterward, they lay quietly, each absorbing the wonder of this experience. Matthew cradled her against him, her head on his shoulder, her curls caressing his bare skin. He idly stroked her arm.

"You might have told me," he accused gently.

"Told you what?" she asked sleepily.

"That you were a virgin."

"Why on earth would you think otherwise?" she asked sharply, sleep no longer a factor.

"I don't know," he said, floundering. "I just . . . you seemed so . . ."

"So what?" she demanded.

"Well . . . knowledgeable?" He felt her stiffen. "When I told you what kind of marriage I wanted, you did say that you knew what it was all about. . . ."

A defensive note crept into his voice and he hated it. God! This was no way to assert himself as her husband. He tried to calm her by caressing her side and belly. She pushed his hand away.

"And you just assumed I gave myself to every man who ever expressed interest in me? Is that it?" Her voice was cold.

"No. That is not it at all." He was becoming annoyed. "You were, after all, promised to Robert. You would not have been the first engaged pair to anticipate the wedding night."

"Well, we did not." She glared at him. "Good heavens! Robert hardly even kissed me. At least, not like you . . ."

"Not like I did? Are you telling me that you never responded to him with the kind of . . . enthusiasm . . . you show me?" There was a note of awed disbelief in his voice.

"No, I did not." Fighting angry tears of embarrassment, she threw back the bedcovers. "This conversation has gone far enough. I shall retire to my own bed now."

"Oh, no, you don't." He grabbed her arm and pulled her back down against him. "You are my wife and you will share my bed."

"I fulfilled my marital duty once tonight. Is that not enough?"

"Duty, was it? You were nearly begging me to get on with it. No, by gad, once is not enough."

She lay there rigid with anger and deeply embarrassed at the truth of what he said. She had been nearly begging him. She kept her head turned away from him, but she was keenly aware of his body everywhere it touched hers and of his arms holding her close.

"Look at me." He pulled her chin around toward him. He saw tears glistening in her eyes. "I misjudged you and I am sorry. When you have thought about it more, perhaps you will understand why I did so."

"I do not think you should count on that happening," she said stubbornly.

"I do count on it, for I have seen you exercise good sense in any number of other instances."

He leaned over and kissed her eyes, licking away her tears. "Come, Sarah. What we have is too good to let a simple mistake ruin it." He ran his hand up and down her body. She did not seem quite so stiff now.

She could feel herself softening, her body responding already to his caress. He planted little kisses all over her face and down her neck to her breasts. With a whimper, she turned to him and surrendered to his persuasion.

She gave herself over to becoming an active participant in their lovemaking, but her mind tucked away the thought, he does not truly believe in me, does he?

# Twelve

Morning dawned without the sun, the long-threatened storm having arrived silently in the night. Snow hurled against the window as Matthew threw open the drapes to welcome meager light. He stirred the still-glowing embers of the fire, added more fuel, then slipped back into the warm bed, trying not to wake his wife. He gazed at her while she slept, her hair disheveled upon the pillow, one hand thrown up by her face—the way a baby sleeps, he thought. She looked innocent and vulnerable, but he knew already innocence and vulnerability were tangled with much stronger traits of character in this woman.

She moaned incoherently and turned over, coming into sudden contact with the wall of flesh that was her husband. Her eyes snapped open and she gazed blankly at him for a moment. Then her expression registered recognition and remembrance. She lowered her gaze and blushed, obviously recalling her abandonment during the night.

"Good morning," he whispered, amused by her reaction.

"Good morning. Is it time to get up?" Her reluctance to leave the warmth of the bed vied with her desire to escape this scene of her embarrassment.

"Not yet." He gathered her to him and snuggled his face against her neck, drinking in the blended scents of the lilac of her hair and body and the musk of their lovemaking. She felt the evidence of his arousal against her thigh as his hands and lips sought to bring her to the same pitch.

"Matthew?"

"Hmmm?"

"Matthew . . . surely you do not mean us to . . . what we did . . . in broad daylight . . . do you?"

"Why not?" He laughed softly.

"Well, it . . . is not proper, I am sure." She sounded very prim.

" 'Proper,' dear wife, is whatever we want, whenever we please in our own chambers."

"But . . . the servants . . ."

"Will come when they are summoned."

"W-w-won't they know what we are doing?"

"I suspect they have a very good idea of what we have been up to all night." He chuckled. "What is more, they probably envy us."

"Oh. . . . You are quite certain this is all right?" She was still doubtful, even as her own desire manifested itself.

"Yes, my dear. Unless you are too sore from before." This thought had suddenly occurred to him and the concern showed in his voice. "Are you?"

She paused. "There is a certain tenderness, but I think I should like to do it again," she said shyly.

And they did.

Twice.

The second time at her initiation, much to his delight.

They finally arose late in the morning to find it still snowing. For two days they were locked in a white world all to themselves, for the roads were impassable. The servants went about their usual business of satisfying basic needs of food, fires, and baths circumspectly, never intruding on the earl and his new countess.

They played piquet and chess. Sarah discovered Trenville was right—they were well matched. They bundled up to visit the stables to check on a new foal which they promptly dubbed "Matty" as short for *matrimony*. Sarah was surprised at the easiness of their relationship. Almost like lovers, she thought, but quickly dismissed that idea.

On the third day, the roads were clear and the world and reality bounded back into their lives.

In late January they journeyed to London. Although the Brocktons would not remove to London for another month, the Markholme party required three carriages to transport themselves, their servants, and their luggage.

They arrived at Markholme House on Mount Street to find the staff, augmented by servants from the country, lined up in the hall, the Londoners eager to assess the new countess. Sarah judged that she came off well initially, for there were smiles and friendly curtsies or bows all round.

The next day Matthew was off to the War Office, taking Charles with him to begin procedures for the younger man to obtain his commission. The ladies spent the better part of the day with a mantua-maker choosing fabrics and styles, as well as being measured and turned this way and that repeatedly.

Having inspected the house with Sarah, Matthew left details of renovation up to her and the housekeeper. He simply retreated, spending his time at the War Office, at his club, or with Trenville, who had also returned to town, riding or attending sporting events. Occasionally, Charles and Hendley joined them.

Spending time at his club or sporting events was all well and good, but Matthew was also determined to learn all he could of the brewery business. He renewed his acquaintance with Whitbread who willingly shared his experiences and expertise. The more he learned, the more enthusiastic Matthew became about establishing a brewery in Derbyshire. He did not, however, share his findings with Sarah. He wanted to wait until he could present his argument, not as a *fait accompli*, but certainly in such forceful terms that she could find little to question.

Since coming to London, Matthew and Sarah had seen little of each other during the day and their evenings were increasingly taken up with social engagements. They formed the agreeable habit of sharing the day's activities over a glass of wine or brandy before they retired. This was their private time and both looked forward to a degree of intimacy that went beyond the lovemaking which continued to present new discoveries and new pleasures.

"I was right, wife," Matthew murmured one night after an especially satisfying encounter.

"About what?" she asked sleepily.

"We do, indeed, suit quite well in this respect."

"Well, just think how awful it could be if we did not." She settled her delectable little bottom in the curve of his legs and body to sleep spoon-fashion.

The *ton* returned to the city for the season and their social obligations intensified. Emily's presentation at court was accomplished with Sarah and Aunt Bess feeling more nervous and jittery than the debutante herself. Cheerful, enthusiastic, and eager to please, Emily took this grand event in stride, as she did most things in her life. This was one of those rare occasions when the Prince Regent was persuaded to attend his mother's reception at which new debutantes were presented to the queen and her daughters.

When it was over, Matthew picked them up and, as the three ladies settled into the carriage, Aunt Bess quizzed Emily.

"What did the Prince say to you, Emily—and what did you say to make him laugh so uproariously?" There was a touch of apprehension in Aunt Bess's tone.

"He said he found such a profusion of beauty and innocence quite charming."

"And you said . . ." prompted Aunt Bess.

"I said I could see how one could judge appearance, but not how one could determine virtue at such an affair."

"Oh, Emily, you did not say anything so forward," Aunt Bess reproved in a shocked tone. Sarah was torn between being appalled and amused. Matthew chuckled softly.

"Well, yes, I did. Was it so very wrong of me?"

"I cannot imagine that Prinny thought anything untoward in it," Matthew said.

"Perhaps not," Aunt Bess replied, "but the ladies of the
court surely did. Really, Emily, you must guard your tongue.
We go to Almack's on Wednesday and you know what stick-
lers for decorum the patronesses are."

"Yes, ma'am." Emily's tone was contrite.

Matthew did not look forward to attending the assembly
at Almack's. In his experience, that redoubtable institution
offered deadly dull entertainment. People went there to
be able to say they had been there, thus conveying the
notion they belonged to the exclusive group granted
vouchers to attend. The food was less than memorable,
drinks insipid, and the atmosphere thick with pomp and
pretension. However, it was the most elite "shop" of the
marriage mart, and it was here that a single young miss
simply had to be seen. It was all rather frivolous and foolish, but the *ton* seemed caught up in that frivolity and foolishness. Who was one Matthew Carey Cameron to go
against society? So, he agreed to escort his womenfolk to
the famous Wednesday night assembly.

There they again encountered Annalisa.

She arrived fashionably late, but not so late as to be shut
out when the doors closed at eleven. Her sea green satin
gown cut low in front, and a length of gauze as a shawl
added a dramatic touch. She always did know how to make
an entrance, Matthew observed.

Standing next to Matthew, but talking with Lady Jersey,
one of the patronesses of Almack's, Sarah noticed him stiff-
en slightly. She turned to see what had so drawn his attention, and noted that, even while Annalisa cavorted with a
court of admirers, she kept glancing toward Matthew.

"Why, yes, I shall see immediately to presenting your
sister a suitable partner for the waltz," Lady Jersey said
and left to carry out that mission.

"One hurdle safely taken, then," Sarah said to Matthew.

"Hmmm? What is that, my dear?"

"Were you not attending, then? Lady Jersey has given permission for Emily to waltz."

"Oh. Just as well. Emily is undoubtedly one of the finest performers in the room."

"As to that, you do not do so badly yourself, my lord. I can testify to your prowess both from my own experience as your partner and from watching you with the lovely Lady Poindexter." Now why did I say that, she asked herself. I sound like a jealous fishwife.

He looked at her questioningly, and as the orchestra even then began the strains of waltz, he opened his arms. "Shall we, my dear?"

Emily joined the set on the arm of a young viscount, Lord Huddleston. She smiled gaily at her sister as they passed each other.

"I see Emily has captured yet another heart," Matthew said observing the smug triumph on the face of her partner.

"It would appear so." Sarah laughed. "Goodness, have you noticed all the bouquets and posies in our entryway?"

"I surely have. Our Emily seems on her way to becoming this season's Incomparable. Do you think she favors any of them yet?" He thought of Hendley and the disappointment that young man was in for.

"None that I am aware of. But I should not want her to feel she must make a choice in any great hurry. She is young yet." She liked the way he had said "our" Emily.

"Huddleston's fortune would certainly recommend him."

"I think his mama keeps him on rather short leading strings, though." Sarah's laughter was a soft gurgle. "Can you imagine such a mama coping with Emily's enthusiasm?"

"You have a point." He paused. "What do you think of Hendley?"

Her answer was abrupt. "Out of the question."

"He seems rather fond of her."

"Perhaps. But a young low-ranking military officer with

few prospects is not exactly a prime article on the marriage mart," she said tartly.

"I see. A Longbourne woman must have rank, title, and fortune, eh? Or at least two of the three." And, he added to himself, Hendley, like another young lieutenant years earlier, had none of these attributes.

Sarah was startled by his sarcastic tone, but before she could frame a response, the dance ended and they returned to the sidelines. Annalisa steered her partner toward them.

"Good evening, Lord Markholme, Lady Markholme." There was only a trace of mockery in her greeting. "Oh, la, Matthew. Imagine you at Almack's." Touching his arm, she smiled at him intimately. "You never used to like it above half. We always arrived just as the doors closed."

"I do not recall." In fact, Matthew knew this was a fabrication, probably for Sarah's benefit. He had rarely attended Almack's and remembered escorting Miss Dalrymple there only once, but one did not accuse a lady of lying.

"Oh, yes." She gave Sarah a conspiratorial wink and continued in a coy tone, "You must know that Matthew and I were quite close once upon a time. Now, of course, we are merely friends. Is it not wonderful that after all this time we are still friends? Do you mind terribly sharing him with his special friends?"

"With his friends? Not at all." Sarah knew any other reply would put her in a bad light.

"You see, Matthew," Annalisa said, smiling directly into his eyes, "I *told* you she would understand. She will have no objection to your dancing with me after all, will you, my lady?" She gave his arm a slight tug.

"No, of course not," Sarah murmured, conscious of the dozens of eyes and not a few ears directed their way.

Matthew was furious. Short of making a scene, he could not refuse to accompany Annalisa to the dance floor. It was a country dance allowing intermittent bits of conversation. She smiled and flirted and simpered. He kept his expression bland, but left no question as to his mood when he spoke.

"That was not well done of you, my lady."

"What?" she asked innocently.

"First off, you know very well I rarely set foot in Almack's when you and I knew each other before."

"Oh, did you not? I thought you had," she said airily.

"And you deliberately led Sarah to think I had been discussing her with you—which you know to be an untruth as well."

"Oh, dear Matthew," she said condescendingly. "Surely you mistake the matter. But I will endeavor to set things aright with your wife if you think she is overly concerned."

"No! You have said quite enough already. I will deal with Sarah myself."

"As you will, my lord." She turned away with a secret smile on her lips. The rest of the dance passed in silence.

Although Sarah seemed attentive to the conversation around her and even contributed to it, she could not afterward have told what the topic of discussion had been. Her mind was fixed on the unfinished conversation with her husband. Something she said had certainly ruffled his feathers. Rank, title, fortune. Surely he understood those were prerequisites for a young lady hunting a husband.

She watched the dancers on the floor, her attention drawn irresistibly to Matthew and his partner. I cannot like that woman, she mused. Nor did it sit well with Sarah that Matthew had apparently shared concerns about his wife with Lady Poindexter. It did not seem in character for him to do so, but Annalisa seemed to know Matthew much more intimately than his wife did.

The rest of the evening passed without further incident, but Matthew found no chance to reintroduce the subject of Hendley and Emily, or to put his wife's mind at ease. That it was not at ease was clear to him, if not to anyone else. She responded to others' commentary, but had become rather quiet overall. In the carriage, Emily bubbled forth in her enthusiastic way and Aunt Bess replied now and then, but neither Matthew nor Sarah said much. Finally, the other two, sensing tension or fatigue in their companions, subsided and they arrived home in comparative silence. There were only brief good nights.

"Sarah . . ." Matthew said as he opened the door to her chamber for her.

"Please, Matthew. I am very tired. Would you mind terribly if we just went to our own beds tonight? I shall be more myself in the morning."

"Of course, if that is your wish." Stiffly polite, he raised her hand to his lips and then stepped down the hall to his own room.

Neither of them slept well that night.

# Thirteen

Until the encounter with Annalisa, Sarah was convinced she and Matthew were growing closer. He seemed as delighted as she in new discoveries of shared interests—chess, ancient history, theater, the works of certain poets. Her soldier-husband was well-versed in a wide range of topics.

For his part, Matthew had known few women who shared his intellectual interests—who were not only quick-witted, but also well-read. Sarah was delightfully opinionated as well, especially regarding society's view of women. The idea that a woman should become the virtual property of some man—her father, guardian, brother, or husband—was "Preposterous!" Women, Sarah asserted, were as capable of running the country as men—history had proved that already.

This conversation took place some days after the evening at Almack's. The morning after that event, Matthew had fully intended to bring up the subject of Annalisa's comments, but refrained from doing so when Sarah maintained a tone of forced cheerfulness and carefully avoided any but the most innocuous topics of discussion. When the rest of the family put in their appearance at breakfast, any opportunity to bring her around to the subject uppermost in his own mind was lost. That afternoon his sister and her family arrived, providing additional distractions.

She welcomed him back to her bed and the crisis—if such it had been—was over. Reluctant to introduce a discordant note, he avoided the issue, privately chastising himself for doing so. On the surface their relationship returned to what it had been before.

Now, it was mid-afternoon. Catherine was in the nursery with the children and others of the family were out. Matthew and Sarah were in the drawing room indulging in a rare moment of quiet. She had taken up a piece of embroidery and he was reading a newspaper. He had shared the editor's criticism of a new pamphlet advocating that women be allowed to own property in their own right. Sarah's "Preposterous!" was her reaction to the editor's objections to women being involved in business affairs.

"I suppose next you will say women should invade the battlefield," Matthew teased from behind his newspaper.

"Well, that is not inconceivable." She resented the superior indulgence of his tone. "After all, Boadicea was a *warrior* queen, was she not?"

"She led half-savage ancient Britons in a few forays against ill-defended Roman enclaves."

"Nevertheless, she reconquered London."

"And butchered all the inhabitants." Matthew put aside his newspaper. "I grant you a woman driven by revenge is probably as fierce as a man, and Boadicea was a powerful person—as much man as woman, I daresay."

"A *woman* capable of leading an army."

"Come now, my dear. Her barbarian band was hardly an *army*. When they encountered the Roman army, which they outnumbered tremendously, the Britons perished by the tens of thousands while the Romans lost only a few hundred. . . . And she committed suicide."

"Her tribesmen were farmers and peasants overwhelmed by well-trained, well-equipped professional soldiers. That does not, in my opinion lessen her achievement," Sarah said firmly. "She stands as proof that a woman can be a leader—even on a battlefield."

"Perhaps . . . but I doubt it could be done in modern warfare."

"Joan of Arc donned armor to inspire her countrymen."

"Nearly four centuries ago! It happens only in ancient history and myth."

"But, Matthew," she said with an exaggerated show of patience, "it is men who are in control and deny women such opportunities." And write the histories, she thought.

"Few women would desire such an opportunity. Most are content to run their households and rear their children. Surely you, dear wife, do not aspire to such a post?"

"No, of course not. That is not the point."

"So, what *is* the point?"

"That women are far more capable than most of your sex accredit them to be."

"Present company excepted, of course."

"Of course!" There was light mockery in her tone, but her thoughts took a more serious turn. He was not yet convinced he had made the right decision in allowing her to handle their estate matters in his absence.

"I will grant you," he continued in a lighter vein, "that most of my sex—especially soldiers—find women somewhat perplexing. And I include myself in the lot. Even great Caesar had troubles in that regard."

"Julius Caesar," she declared, "may have been a great soldier and governor, but he was a ninny where women were concerned. And just why is it that so many great military men seem incapable of dealing with women? Word is that Napoleon has certainly not been immune to such problems—and, for an example closer to home, one need only consider the scandalous liaison between Lord Nelson and Lady Hamilton a few years ago. . . ."

Her voice trailed off and she looked away, embarrassed as it dawned on her this mild harangue might be getting very close to home, indeed. An uncomfortable silence fell. Finally, she lifted her gaze to his questioning eyes.

"Did you have another military man even closer at hand in mind, my dear?" His tone was serious, but controlled.

"No. Matthew, I did not mean . . . that is, I was speaking only in general terms . . . please do not think that I . . .

oh, dear. Sometimes I talk too much." The words tumbled out, spilling over each other.

"I thought you perhaps had Lady Poindexter and her unfortunate remarks at Almack's in mind."

"Her unfortunate remarks?" she repeated blankly in a bid for time to think.

"Yes. I suspect she intended you to believe that you had been the subject of some discussion between her and me."

"Well, to be honest, that is what I thought."

He sat forward in his chair and clasped his hands in front of him. "Sarah, please believe me—I do not and will not discuss our life or our marriage with anyone but you."

"Then Lady Poindexter was . . ."

"Exaggerating." He still could not call the woman a liar, though he was annoyed and angered by her attempt to upset Sarah.

"Oh." She looked at him searchingly for a moment. "Thank you, Matthew. I appreciate your concern for my feelings, but really, you need not explain your every move to me. I understand the need for privacy and control of one's own life. Now, if you will excuse me, I must speak with Cook." She rose and hastily left the room.

Now what the hell did that mean, he asked himself. Did she assume he was having an affair with Lady Poindexter? Would she care if he were? If she did think he was involved with another woman, would his equality-minded wife feel permitted to seek attentions elsewhere?

A picture of Sarah entangled in the arms of another man invaded his musings and brought a wave of possessiveness. He found himself foolishly infuriated over something that was, as yet, purely a matter of his own imagination.

Sarah invented the errand to the kitchen to avoid further discussion with Matthew. Such behavior was out of character for one quite used to facing her problems head on, but there was too much at stake to force a confrontation.

Theirs was a marriage of convenience. Emotional demands would violate the unspoken boundaries of their agreement. Matthew said he had not discussed his wife or his marriage with another, and she believed him. But he had not denied a liaison with Lady Poindexter. Was there something to her innuendoes? If so, it had not hit the gossip mill yet. Sarah was certain of that, for surely someone of Lady Meridon's ilk would have been only too glad to toss a hint here and there into a social call. Silence in the gossip mill proved discretion, not abstinence.

And it was discretion Matthew had promised along with his marriage proposal.

He was living up to his end of their bargain; she would strive to fulfill hers as well. The situation would be vastly different if *we were in love with each other,* she thought. *To allow oneself to fall into a one-sided attachment is the way of madness. It cannot be.* She steeled herself against such folly.

Surely, if she put her mind to it, she could ignore the little flip her heart did when he entered a room. The coolly independent Sarah Longbourne would just have to take charge of her own person. . . . But could Lady Markholme forget that her husband's caresses set her on fire?

To avoid confronting her dilemma, she filled her days and their evenings with activities, using the excuse of exposing Emily advantageously on the marriage mart. Alone with Matthew, she introduced no topic that could lead to their exploring their feelings for each other, though she welcomed his sexual overtures. After all, was it not imperative that they conceive an heir? So far, it had not happened, but the attempts were anything but unpleasant.

Matthew was frankly confused. They did not quarrel, but neither did they go beyond the superficial. In company, his wife was polite and charming, but somewhat reserved. In private, she was essentially the same. He felt the presence of a defensive barrier he could not penetrate. Yet she was as warm, passionate, and sharing in their bed as any man could desire. He felt himself inordinately lucky in that regard. In fact, given the conditions of this marriage, he should be immensely satisfied.

But somehow he was not.

London—indeed, all of England—was in the throes of one of the coldest winters on record. Roads often impassable, horses floundered in deep frozen ruts or on ice-covered cobblestones. The Thames froze over. Ordinary communication and commerce came to a standstill.

News from the continent, however, was generally uplifting. In the Peninsula, Wellington, along with his Spanish and Portuguese allies, had the French troops on the run. Napoleon was besieged from all sides. It seemed only a matter of time until he no longer presented the terrible threat he had posed for nearly two decades.

An air of festivity and gaiety prevailed in Markholme House. The season had not properly started yet, but Emily had already established herself as a "diamond of the first water." She flirted outrageously, but never seemed to favor a special beau. If her heart was drawn to one particular red-coated member of His Majesty's Forces, only she was aware of it.

On a cold, clear day in February, the entire Markholme household turned out for the Frost Fair which had materialized on the frozen river, complete with ice-skating and kiosks selling food and drink. The winter sun was weak, but the air was amazingly free of the usual dense fog of a London winter. Small puffs of cloud punctuated conversation and laughter. The Brockton children, bundled up like small bears, frolicked in the snow and ice with their elders.

Sarah stood upon the bank, her skates slung over her shoulder, and watched. Edward and Catherine skated on either side of young Ned, and Matthew had taken the ice with little Katie-Ann. Emily's merry laughter rang out, taunting the two young men pursuing her. The solid stage of the river had turned into a ballroom of graceful dancers.

A sense of contentment washed over her, and catching

sight of Matthew, she thought about the changes he had brought to her life. Her family circle had grown to include wonderful new friends. Charles would have his commission and Emily would make a suitable match. Whatever might have happened to us, had Matthew not arrived on our scene?

As if on cue, he appeared before her, having turned over his charge to her mother. He smiled and held out a gloved hand.

"Come Sarah. We will show them how it should be done. Let me help you." He led her to a bench and took her skates from her. Removing his gloves, he knelt before her to fit the blades to her boots. "We have been here before, have we not?" He laughed up at her. "Only this time your ankle is in perfect order." He surreptitiously caressed her leg.

"Matthew!" The laughter in her voice belied the admonishment as she pushed his hand away and readjusted the hem of her cloak. He grinned, put his gloves back on, and led her onto the ice.

They skated smoothly and sedately together for a round or two. Then, gaining momentum and enthusiasm, they twirled and danced on the ice, their movements becoming faster and more intricate. Having, indeed, shown the others, they graciously acknowledged a round of applause and continued.

Unable to suppress a gurgle of laughter, Sarah was happily startled to see her exhilaration mirrored in his eyes. And something else—naked hunger that sent a surge of warmth swirling through her. She caught her breath, and promptly missed her step, missed catching his hand. She stumbled awkwardly, trying to maintain her balance and fleetingly noted that missing her hand had set Matthew off balance as well, though he stayed on his feet. Suddenly on her bottom, she sailed across the ice toward the near bank.

The fall knocked the breath out of her and she lay on the ice a moment, stunned.

"Sarah!" Matthew glided over to gather her in his arms.

"Are you hurt? Please, my love, speak to me," he murmured into her hair.

She took a couple of deep breaths. "I . . . am . . . fine," she panted. "Just help me up, please."

He guided her over to the bench on which she had sat earlier. "Are you sure you are all right?"

"Yes, I am sure. I just need to catch my breath. Please do not refine upon it, Matthew. We will spoil the others' enjoyment."

"Hang the others," he said, peevishly. Then, seeing the amusement in her eyes, he was slightly embarrassed. "I will get you some hot cider." He skated off and returned shortly with a steaming cup in his hand which they shared in companionable silence, watching the other skaters.

"You know, that was all your fault," she said.

"My fault? How did you arrive at that interesting conclusion?"

"If you had not looked at me like that, I would not have misstepped."

"Like what?" He grinned.

"You know very well 'like what.' "

"Yes, but I want to hear you say it," he whispered, leaning close and brushing her cheek lightly with his lips.

She turned to look directly into his eyes. "You are doing it again," she breathed.

"I fear you are doing the same, dear wife." The caress in his voice was accompanied by his arm around her waist.

Catherine's voice broke in on them as she came up holding her daughter's hand. "Sarah. Are you all right? That was a nasty spill you took."

"I am fine." Sarah, not at all sure she welcomed the intrusion, knew it was just as well it had occurred before she said or did something foolish. "Katie-Ann, would you like to sit with Aunt Sarah while Mama and Uncle Matthew take a turn about the ice?" She extended her arms to the child who readily came into them.

"I think the woman wants to be rid of me," Matthew joked to his sister over his wife's head.

"Yes. She appeared to be desperately fighting for her life and virtue as we approached." Catherine laughed. "Come on, big brother. Skate with me." She pulled him to his feet and the two of them took to the ice.

"Mmm. You smell good." Sarah nuzzled the little girl's cold cheek and hugged her close.

"So do you, Auntie Sarah," the child said seriously.

Is this how it will feel to hold Matthew's child?

The idea was at once comforting and unsettling. Comforting, for she did long for a child of her own. Unsettling, because a child would symbolize a union that did not really exist between her and Matthew. However, she told herself pragmatically, getting an heir is one of the reasons for this union, is it not?

Then another thought occurred to her. He called me his love, she reflected wonderingly. It would not do to dwell on that, now, would it?

That night when Matthew invited Sarah into the huge four-poster bed of the master chamber, she went eagerly. Their lovemaking fulfilled the unspoken promises of the afternoon and each felt they had come a long way toward regaining the understanding they enjoyed in those first days of their marriage.

The next day, Major Cameron and Lieutenant Hendley were called back to duty.

# Fourteen

Adult members of the household were still at breakfast when Wendell, the London butler, presented a card on a salver to Lord Markholme. Matthew looked at the name, then quickly excused himself.

Instinctively, Sarah knew it was the long-awaited message from the War Office. Her heart sank at the thought that Matthew would leave soon. Conversation at the table had been lively and light. Now the others, sensing her disquiet, grew more subdued.

Presently the butler returned and said softly to Sarah, "His lordship asks that you join him in the library, my lady, at your convenience." She found Matthew standing in front of the fireplace where a feeble blaze failed to lend much warmth to the room.

"It has come," he said simply. "I am to report to Wellington in the south of France 'with all due expedience.' Hendley and several others will accompany me."

"Oh, Matthew." She put her hand to her mouth to still her trembling lips. "When?"

"A few days. A week at most. Ships are being readied in Portsmouth."

"I thought I was prepared for your leaving, but it comes as a shock. We . . . I shall miss you." Unshed tears added a silvery shine to the violet of her eyes.

"And I you." He pulled her into his arms and they stood clinging to each other, each drawing strength from the sheer physical presence of the other. "But I am not gone yet. We have a few days."

"There is so much to do . . ."

"Yes. And we had best get started." He reluctantly pulled away, but kissed her lightly before releasing her.

He opened the door and instructed a footman to send Coop to him. When that worthy man had presented himself, Matthew gave him the merest outline of their orders, knowing Coop would see to everything. The same footman was then sent round to Hendley's quarters with a note asking him to call at Markholme House.

Despite frequent outings with any number of young gentlemen, Emily had, without conscious consideration, grown closer to Richard Hendley. Exhibiting youth's usual propensity to live for the moment, she thought little of his return to the war. She enjoyed his quiet humor, his caring concern, his willingness to go along with her schemes—even his voice of common sense and restraint. She was more likely to share a private, serious moment with him than with another, but he belonged to a group with whom she laughed and danced and played youth's eternal games.

At the very advanced age of twenty-two, Hendley adopted a demeanor of stoic acceptance, for he knew very well his own value on the marriage mart. He was fond of the girl, but she was, after all, in her first season and needed to spread her wings, as it were. Meanwhile, Emily seemed in no hurry to secure an attachment and he enjoyed watching her embrace all that life offered.

Responding to Matthew's summons, Richard presented himself at Markholme House to receive the long-anticipated news. His first thought was to secure an audience with Emily. A short while later, they strolled casually in the garden at the rear of the house.

"Have you heard the news?" he asked.

"You and Matthew will return to the Peninsula? Yes."

"Seems hardly worth the effort now that Boney is more or less on the run on the rest of the continent."

"I thought you were eager to return to the fray."

"I was," he said defensively, "so long as it seemed there was a real need for us. Wellington may be on his way home by the time we arrive back there."

"Oooh," she teased, "is the lowly lieutenant daring to question the wisdom of his superiors?"

He grinned. "I could not do that, now could I? But there is the war in America, too. I might have gone there."

"Are you so bent on fighting or killing that just any war will do for you?" Her tone was light, but there was a serious edge to it.

He paused and she automatically stopped, too, and turned toward him.

"I think you know me better than that, Emily. One gains advancement much more rapidly on the battlefield than rusticating in a peacetime army."

"And you are so ambitious for quick advancement?"

He chose his words carefully. "Some day I may want to marry and have a family. I could not ask a woman to share my life as it is now."

"That would depend on the woman, would it not?"

"I saw women in Spain and Portugal struggle to follow their men in the army. They endure incredible hardships. I simply could not ask anyone to do that for me."

"Perhaps she would not be doing it *for you,* but in order that the two of you could build something together." Emily was more serious than he had ever seen her before.

"It is simply not the sort of life one could ask a blooming flower of English society to share."

"Some of England's flowers are of hardier stock than you give them credit for." She turned and walked on.

"Still, I could have wished for another assignment."

"Or," she said too brightly, "you could solve all your problems by hanging out for a rich heiress."

He snorted. "Has it escaped your notice that rich heiresses are not likely to look with favor on lowly, penniless lieutenants?"

"Well, then, a rich widow who need not concern herself with titles and such in a second husband. One who would welcome a fine *young* specimen such as you." Emily laughed.

"I will not be bought," he said loftily. "It is all well and good for you to hold out for some rich old curmudgeon with a title, if you must—"

She stopped, her cheeks flushed with anger. "What did you say?" She fairly hissed at him.

"I said—"

"Never mind. I heard you and I think that is decidedly the most idiotic thing ever to come from your mouth. How wonderful that you credit yourself with a higher moral sensibility than you are willing to credit me. You have a nice opinion of me, have you not?" She turned back into the house.

In high dudgeon, she stormed up the stairs, presumably to her own chamber. Close behind her came Hendley just as Matthew entered the hallway from the library.

"Emily, wait!" Seeing Matthew, he threw up his hands helplessly and shrugged. "Women!" he muttered.

"Little problem with the fair sex?" Matthew asked sympathetically.

"You might say that."

"Want to tell Uncle Matthew all about it?"

"Not just yet, sir," Hendley said stiffly.

Out on the street a few minutes later, he muttered about the perfidy of women—in particular, about pretty little blondes who deliberately misunderstood a fellow.

Matthew tried without success—and finally without much enthusiasm for his argument—to dissuade Sarah from seeing him off at Portsmouth. Emily accompanied her sister, along with a maid and sufficient outriders for the ladies' return trip. The journey to the port had taken three days for a trip Matthew, Hendley, and Coop might have achieved in half the time, but the extra days with Sarah had been worth it. This night, at an inn near the harbor, was their last night.

Matthew joined Sarah in their room to freshen up before going to dinner in the private parlor they had reserved.

"You are looking especially fine this evening, my dear," he said, placing his hands on her shoulders and bending close. Seated at a dressing table, she was wearing a gown of deep rose trimmed with black piping.

"Thank you, Matthew." She caught his eye in the looking glass, then lowered her gaze shyly. "I wanted to make our last night a little special."

"It will be. I promise you." There was a wicked glint in his eyes as his hands caressed her shoulders and neck. He watched her face in the glass as his fingers lightly swept the tops of her breasts above the low-cut neckline of her gown.

"Matthew!" She pushed his hand away, pretending to be shocked, but the initial intake of breath had given her away. He chuckled and turned to his own preparations.

"Do you think our young friend and your saucy sister have resolved their differences yet?" Matthew asked as he adjusted his waistcoat.

"I think not. Emily has been very quiet for several days—strange for her, you know. And they have not really had a chance to do so, as they have taken their meals with us and Richard seems glued to that infernal horse of his."

"I invited him to join us." Matthew had ridden with the ladies in the carriage for a good portion of each day. Hendley had declined invitations to share their comfort.

"It is just as well he refused you," Sarah said firmly. "Emily should make a better match than is offered in that quarter. I had hoped that this journey would be a bit more enjoyable for her. Now I feel guilty for insisting on her company."

"Your objection to Hendley is not personal, is it?"

"No. Of course not. He is a fine, engaging young man, but Emily has no fortune and neither does he. She should look elsewhere for a suitable match."

Matthew suspected the young people's feelings went beyond the question of a "suitable match," but he deliberately chose not to take issue with his wife's position. Especially not now, on the eve of their parting. What will be will be.

In the private parlor they found Hendley sipping a glass of sherry. He rose to greet them.

"Ah, Lady Markholme, you are in especially good looks this evening." He bowed over her hand.

"I thought we had agreed on 'Sarah' and 'Richard' lo these many weeks ago," she reproved.

"So we had. But you must know that being in the august presence of my commanding officer forces me into more formal means of address."

"Hendley . . ." Matthew fairly growled at him and the younger man grinned at him.

"Emily has not come in yet?" Sarah asked to change the subject.

"I think she is still avoiding me and wished to ensure you were here before she arrived," Hendley said.

"Sherry, my dear?" Matthew asked, pouring for the two of them when she said, "Please."

"Hello, everyone." Emily's cheerful voice sounded from the doorway.

"The princess arrives at last," Hendley muttered just under his breath. Emily cast him a fulminating look.

Hard on Emily's heels came the innkeeper and one of his maids with their dinner, a simple meal of white fish followed by roast lamb and vegetables and ending with an apple tart. Conversation was cordial, despite the undercurrent of animosity between the younger diners, each of whom was too well-reared to make a general issue of their disagreement.

"I enjoyed that," Matthew announced at the end of the meal, "but I fear I need to work a bit of it off before retiring. What say we all take a walk along the sea wall? 'Tis cold out there, but the weather is clear."

"I should like that," Sarah said. "Just let me get my cloak. Emily?"

"Yes," Emily said, rising.

Having secured suitable outdoor attire, the foursome met again in the parlor. As they stepped out the inn door, Matthew made a point of offering his arm to his wife, leaving Emily and Hendley no choice but to walk together.

Hendley politely offered Emily his arm which she took as though it were a hot poker. Matthew motioned the younger couple to go ahead.

"Perhaps they will sort themselves out," he said softly to Sarah, encouraging her to walk more slowly to put distance between themselves and the others.

"Perhaps," Sarah said, "but Emily can be very stubborn. It is a family trait, you know." The moon reflecting off the sea provided enough light for him to see her sheepish smile.


Emily was not ready to forgive her sometime swain. If Richard Hendley expected her to accept him back into her good graces any time soon, he was whistling in the wind. She walked beside him stiffly, but totally aware of the muscled forearm under her hand.

Richard cleared his throat. "Are you still angry?"

"Why should I not be?"

"It was such a trivial thing, after all—"

"Trivial! You accuse me of being a fortune hunter, and now you have the audacity to label the matter trivial?" She tried to pull her hand from his arm, but he quickly caught it with his other hand and refused the separation.

They came to a stairway leading to the beach and he guided her down the steps. At the bottom, he swung her around so her back was against the wall and his gloved palms flat against it on either side of her shoulders.

"Emily, please. You know very well that was not exactly what I meant."

"Well, that is exactly what you said," she retorted, not looking at him.

"I know it did not come out very well, but I only meant to point out what we both know—you must make an advantageous marriage. It is just that I . . . I care about you . . . and as your friend, I would hate to see you—"

"You just listen to me, Richard Hendley," she interrupted fiercely. She looked squarely at him, glad the bright moonlight allowed her to see him clearly. She measured each word carefully. "I shall never marry where there is no affection. Never."

He looked at her silently a moment. "I am glad to hear you say that."

"It is not just words, you know." Her tone softened.

"I did not suppose it was." Encouraged, he moved even closer and slid his hands to her shoulders. "Ah, Emily, let us not part on a sour note. I do not want to go off to France with you thinking ill of me." He gave her a brotherly peck on her brow.

"No," she breathed, turning her face up, her lips slightly parted.

Their gazes locked and as the silence lengthened, she licked her lips nervously. He lowered his mouth to hers in a most unbrotherly manner. Her response, at first tentative, intensified. He was the first to pull away.

"Lord, I had no right to do that. I'm sorry, Emily," he whispered.

"I am not sorry at all," she said frankly. Then, irrepressible as ever, she added, "You know, that was my first real kiss. I quite liked it."

He grinned. "Still, it should not have happened . . . though I am glad you liked it. Come, we had best get back to the others."

# Fifteen

Having dismissed their respective servants, Matthew and Sarah were preparing for bed.

"That was not very subtle of you, my lord."

"But it worked, did it not?" He refused to pretend to misunderstand. "They finished the walk in charity with each other—to the point that Emily would probably still be in the parlor entertaining Hendley with some *on dit* or other had you not pointedly suggested it was bedtime and sent her off to join Betsy."

"Still . . . I cannot think it wise to encourage them."

"Good lord, Sarah, they are young. They enjoy each other's company."

"Young lieutenants have been known to fall in love without much regard to the harsher realities of life, have they not?" she asked gently.

Removing his neckcloth, Matthew paused and shot her a piercing look.

"True," he said tersely. He tossed the neckcloth on a chair and unbuttoned his waistcoat.

Sarah was immediately sorry she had asked the question. Things were going so well—and here she introduced a discordant note. She struggled with the buttons on the back of her gown. She would have to dismiss Betsy when she was trussed up like a Christmas goose!

"True," he repeated, "but some young lieutenants have a more realistic view of their world than others may have

had. Hendley is well aware of his shortcomings on the marriage mart." He paused and then added, "Besides, I did
not want him going into battle feeling as he was before.
That could be dangerous."

"But Emily has had so little experience . . ."

"Put your mind at ease, Sarah. Richard is a thoroughly
honorable young man. He has been with me for nearly five
years now. I have never seen him take advantage of a
woman. And believe me, it was not for lack of opportunity!"

"Oh? And did higher-ranking officers enjoy similar opportunities?" she teased, obviously dropping the topic of
her sister and his subaltern.

"Occasionally." He grinned at her reflection in the
cheval glass as she twisted into interesting contortions in
an effort to gain access to the buttons on her gown. "Here.
Allow me." He strode over to make quick work of the task.
He bent to touch his lips to the nape of her neck and
wound his arms tightly around her. He inhaled the delicate
lilac mixed with a tantalizing scent that was purely Sarah.

"Before you distract me completely, woman—do you
want me to speak to Hendley?" His breath on her ear, not
to mention his caressing hands, sent frissons of desire
throughout her body.

"No-o-o." She drew the word out as she tried to focus
on the discussion. "I think not. His leaving tomorrow and
her return to the season's festivities will probably spell the
end of it."

Feeling deliciously decadent, she watched the very male
image in the looking glass slide the gown off the shoulders
of an eager female image, and felt the folds of cloth en-
circle her feet. She twisted in his arms to face him, entwine
her hands in the soft curls at the back of his neck, and
give herself up to the headiness of a deep kiss.

He nudged her toward the bed which had been turned
back earlier. Quickly divesting himself of his remaining
garments, he reached to douse the candle on the bedside
table.

"No," she said. "Please, I want to see you."

He chuckled and assumed statue-like poses to tease her.

"You are so beautiful," she whispered seriously.

"That is supposed to be the man's line, my dear." Embarrassed by her frank admiration, he leaned over to kiss her again. He lay beside her and pulled her close.

"It is true, Matthew."

"If so," he murmured doubtfully, "we are indeed well matched, my dear, for you are incredibly lovely."

Their lovemaking took on a desperate sense of urgency; the intensity tempered by tenderness. The prospect of tomorrow's separation made each of them determined that tonight's union should be sheer perfection.

And it was.

Afterward, Matthew raised himself on his elbows to look into her face. Tears squeezed from the corners of her closed eyes.

"Sarah? Did I hurt you?"

She opened her eyes, twin wells of violet still deepened by passion. "No, Matthew. It was just so wonderful. I never dreamed our marriage would be so . . . so . . ."

"Satisfying?"

"Yes. And . . . more. I feel so complete with you. I am going to miss you so much."

It was true. He was an integral part of her life. Not just as a player in the routine of their day-to-day activities or as a partner in the business of their estates and investments. No. It was more than that. He seemed almost a part of her personal, emotional self. There would be such emptiness on the morrow. But she had already said too much. Emotional involvement was not part of their bargain. . . . Or was that part of the bargain changing? Had he not called her his love again?

Matthew kissed her tenderly and rolled over to the side, keeping her within the private little world of his arms.

God! Cameron, how did you get so damned lucky? Her passion never ceased to surprise him. Who would ever suspect that this cool, efficient woman would be such a passionate, sensual delight? Sexual encounters had always been just that for him—sex that allowed a sense of physical release and little else.

With Sarah it was so much more. . . .

The next morning, Matthew was annoyed with himself for giving in to Sarah's insistence that she and Emily see them off at the dock. But last night he would have—could have—refused her nothing. Coop took care of getting equipment and luggage on board, except for the dispatch case Matthew kept with him all the time. The carriage was loaded to take the women back to London as soon as the ship sailed. Betsy was temporarily relegated to the driver's perch as the two couples occupied the interior of the coach.

They did not talk much, and when they did, it was to repeat mundane instructions or to make comments totally unrelated to the imminent parting.

"You will not forget to contact Whitbread, now will you?" Matthew asked. Their clasped hands were only partially concealed by the folds of her cloak.

"No, of course not," Sarah replied. "Are you sure you have enough warm clothing? Nights can be cold even in spring."

"Why are there so many women and children here?" Emily asked as they approached the dock.

"Most of them were hoping to go along with their husbands and fathers," Matthew said.

"On board a troop ship? You cannot be serious," Emily expostulated.

"Yes," he replied. "For each one hundred soldiers, six women are allowed to accompany an army unit. They may or may not have their children with them."

"But—but where do they live on board? Where do they eat and sleep? Do they have proper accommodations?" Emily was openly intrigued by the logistics.

Matthew and Richard both chuckled.

"You tell her, Richard," Matthew said.

"They live with their men," Hendley said matter-offactly. "They get half as much in rations as their husbands get, though husbands usually share. They sleep in the same quarters as their men."

"You mean . . . they have no privacy at all?" Clearly, Emily could hardly believe what she was hearing.

"None at all," Matthew said.

"I told you, did I not, that women truly suffered in the Peninsula?" Hendley's I-told-you-so tone would have done a boy of ten proud. "And they will live in tents and crude huts in the field, too."

Emily bit her lower lip thoughtfully for a moment. "It must take a very powerful love to persuade a woman to endure such a life."

No one said anything for a minute or two. Matthew squeezed Sarah's hand tightly.

"How do they decide which women will go?" Sarah asked, observing couples and little family groups gathered on the dock.

Matthew leaned across his wife to peer out the window. "By lot. They probably assembled this morning and each woman drew a piece of paper with 'to go' or 'not to go' written on it. Of course, there are far more 'not to gos.' "

"You can tell by looking at their faces which were the lucky 'to go' winners." Sarah's voice was soft at his ear.

He turned to look at her wonderingly, their faces nearly touching. Cocking his hat to shield them, however ineffectually, he quickly pressed his lips to hers, then settled back to his own share of the seat. Emily giggled and Hendley grinned at the surprised look on Sarah's face. When she turned to glare at Matthew, he just looked smug.

There was a festive air about the three ships being readied to sail with the tide. Hauling horses and huge bales of goods on board required much jostling and shouting. Young soldiers stood around in their own groups, playfully jabbing at each other, then looking to see if their antics were getting any attention, especially from females in the crowd. Sarah concluded that many of them had drunk their breakfast. But who could blame them? For how many would this be their last sight of home?

"Major Cameron! I say, sir, 'tis good to see you with us!" The greeting came from a burly sergeant standing with a sturdy-looking woman.

"MacGowan! How are you?" Matthew extended his hand warmly. "And what are you doing here? I left you wallowing in a ditch in Portugal."

"That you did, sir. But then I caught a bullet and I've been home a'mendin' these four months or more. Guess they can't get the Frenchies without me, though, 'cause they tell me I'm ready ta go back."

"Good sergeants are hard to come by," Matthew said sincerely.

"This time Maggie's comin' with me," MacGowan said, pulling his wife forward and making her known to the major.

"Mrs. MacGowan." Matthew tipped his hat to acknowledge the introduction. "I am sure you will keep him in line for us. May I present my wife, Lady Markholme?"

"Pleased, your ladyship," the husband and wife murmured in unison, executing a slight bow and curtsy.

"Tommy says as how you saved his bacon on more than one occasion, my lord," Mrs. MacGowan said warmly to Matthew, "and I told him if'n I ever got a chance, I would sure thank you for that—an' I do."

Matthew looked embarrassed. "Oh. Well. As I said, good sergeants are hard to come by."

"Maggie, darlin', we'd best get on now," MacGowan said, drawing his wife away with a polite nod to the Markholmes.

Sarah clung tightly to Matthew's arm and noted that Emily kept hold of Hendley's as the dock became more crowded and the activity more frenzied. They were jostled repeatedly.

"You see?" Matthew said, not ungently, and holding her hand tightly against his body. "I told you it would be chaos down here. You would be better to have stayed at the inn—or started your own journey earlier."

"I would not have missed this—or the last three days—for the world."

"Only the days?" Matthew raised one eyebrow in his familiar way.

Just as he had intended, she colored up at this remark. He smiled at her and moved his hand to rest loosely around her shoulders.

"Ah, my Sarah. Will you blush so delightfully when we are both decrepit oldsters, my dear?"

"If you continue to make improper remarks to me in public, my lord," she said in mock umbrage, her eyes twinkling, "you will be very lucky to get to be an oldster, decrepit or otherwise!"

Suddenly the scene around them and the implications of what she had said hit her. She drew in a sharp breath and put her fingers to her mouth. "I did not mean . . ."

"Don't say it. Don't even think it, my dear." His hand tightened on her shoulder. "I will return shortly. You can get yours back then. I *will* return, Sarah. Never fear."

Looking at him bleakly, she accepted his vow for what it was—a solemn promise to return to her. She put her arm around his waist and hugged him. Such a public display of affection was highly improper, but she did not care.

Moments later, Coop was at Matthew's elbow. "The ship's captain says as how he's ready for ye, my lord. An' I'll be biddin' ye goodbye, my lady." He pulled at his cap.

Sarah offered the older man her hand. "Coop. You take good care of him, now—and yourself as well." She gripped his hand fiercely.

"I will, my lady. That I will." He patted her hand reassuringly.

"I must go," Matthew said. "Please do not wait now. The ship will not sail for another hour or more and there is nothing more for you to see or do here."

"All right. I will just wait to see that you are on board. Then we will go." A boulder blocked the back of her throat and tears blurred her vision.

"Don't, sweetheart. Please, don't." He pulled her head to his shoulder.

"I'm sorry." She took a deep breath and swallowed. She

looked up at him and there were only the two of them alone on the crowded dock. He bent and touched his lips firmly and lingeringly to hers without regard to the audience surrounding them. Then he was gone, making his way toward the gangplank.

Hendley had entertained Emily with outrageous tales of stubborn mules and English soldiers in amusing encounters with Spanish and Portuguese peasants. Seeing Matthew move toward the ship, he said, "Well, it looks like we are off. You will enjoy the rest of the season, won't you?"

"I shall dance 'til dawn every night," she said too brightly. "And I will write you of all the balls and routs you will be missing."

"You do that." He touched her lightly on the cheek.

"Richard . . . be careful, please."

She rose on her toes, kissed him quickly on the cheek, and turned immediately toward Sarah. She did not see the awed look in his eyes or the hand that went to his cheek.

Sarah and Emily waited for Matthew and Richard to wave at them from the ship's deck, then they turned reluctantly back to the carriage. By the time they stopped for the evening, they had regained their customary poise and interest in their surroundings.

"Sharing a room with me and Betsy is not quite the same as sharing one with Matthew, is it?" Emily asked conversationally, then blushed at what she had said.

"No. It surely is not," Sarah said ruefully. "But all the same, I am glad—very glad—that you are here." She gave her sister a hard hug.

"Me, too. At first I did not want to come, you know. Now, I'm glad I was able to put things right with Richard. It is difficult to be estranged from a friend."

"I know."

Sarah knew she should warn Emily away from the young lieutenant with few prospects—or at least find out the state of affairs between them—but at the moment she was just too caught up in her own jarring reaction to her husband's leave-taking to deal with another problem.

# Sixteen

With the London season in full swing, Sarah plunged into social activities. Her plan to keep herself so busy she would not be preoccupied with Matthew worked during the day—mostly. At night, though, his absence was an aching void. She missed just having him near—beside her on the street, at meals, in the library, in their bed.

"Matthew Carey Cameron, you wretch! You sweet, wonderful, heart-stealing wretch. How is it that you have become such an all-consuming obsession with me?"

Sleepless one night in Matthew's big lonely bed, she lay staring at the underside of the canopy illuminated but faintly by the light from the hearth. Since returning to London, she slept in his bed simply because it made her feel closer to him. Finally, she admitted to herself the unthinkable.

She was in love with her husband.

It was not just that they were compatible in this bed, or that they had formed a friendship based on mutual interests and respect. No matter that they had entered into a contract based on shared material needs. She was wildly, passionately, quietly, and firmly in love with him.

Matthew must never know she had overstepped the limits of their agreement. Maybe someday the affection he showed her would blossom into feelings closer to her own. Maybe. Until then, she refused to become the object of his—or anyone's—pity for bestowing love where it was not returned.

The next day two unfortunate events occurred to send her spirits spiraling downward.

The first was irrefutable proof offered by her own body that she was not with child. She had hoped the frequency and intensity of their intimacy prior to Matthew's departure would result in her becoming pregnant. But she had not. I am not yet satisfying even that part of our agreement, she thought disconsolately.

The second was that she encountered Annalisa Poindexter again. She had seen the woman since returning to London, but this occasion was a small gathering and Annalisa sought Sarah out deliberately.

"Ah, Lady Markholme, may I present my cousin, Sir Hamilton Ridgeley to you?" She brought the man forth without waiting for Sarah to respond.

A handsome man in his early forties, Ridgeley had blond hair with barely noticeable streaks of gray. Startling dark brows framed equally dark eyes. He fought the inevitably losing battle against age more successfully than most. He dressed more fashionably than most, as well.

"It was presumptuous of me, my lady, but I simply had to meet such a beautiful lady. I am told that you share a special interest of mine in modern poetry."

"Well, certain modern poets recommend themselves, I think," Sarah replied. "I cannot like Mr. Wordsworth overmuch, though some of his shorter lyrics are quite nice."

"And Byron?"

"I quite enjoy his work. He has a marvelous sense of humor and an unerring ear for language."

"Byron is a particular friend of mine," he said. "I should be glad to introduce you. He is not really the scoundrel the *on dits* make him out to be."

"Hardly anyone could be as sensational as the gossips have Lord Byron to be," Sarah said.

"Caroline Lamb has not exactly been the soul of discretion where he is concerned," Annalisa put in. "One should conduct such liaisons with more finesse—do you not agree, Lady Markholme?"

"I suppose so," Sarah said, not caring to pursue this topic. "However, if everyone acted according to wisdom, what would the rest of us talk about?"

"The lady herself has a sense of humor," Ridgeley said with a laugh.

"Do you hear from Matthew?" Annalisa asked casually.

"A hurried letter while he was still on board ship."

"Well, I suppose there is little enough to prompt him to write," Annalisa said. "When he first went to the Peninsula, he was a prolific correspondent, you know."

"No. I did not know. But then I did not even know Lord Markholme then," Sarah said stiffly. She could not resist adding, "I was still in the schoolroom, of course."

"Of course." Annalisa's voice was frosty, her eyes hard. "Excuse me. I must speak with Lady Carrington."

"Touché, my lady," Ridgeley said softly when Annalisa was out of hearing.

"That was petty and ill-mannered of me. I am sorry I did that and sorrier that you witnessed it."

" 'Twas only human, I think." He changed the subject.

The next day Sarah received a bouquet of flowers that rivalled one or two of those addressed to Emily. The card simply said, "To a fellow lover of poetry." The following day Ridgeley called to invite Sarah and her companion for a drive in the park. Knowing her aunt would welcome such an outing, Sarah readily accepted.

Hamilton Ridgeley was an amiable, entertaining conversationalist and his conduct was all that was correct. Sarah discovered they had mutual acquaintances and interests and were frequently invited to the same social affairs. He often asked her to dance, but he was invariably proper in his behavior. He was welcomed when he called at Markholme House, though Sarah never received him alone.

Ridgeley introduced Sarah to his poet friend. Impressed with her knowledge of literature in general, Byron was truly taken with her when she quoted passages of his own work to him. She was invited to attend a literary reading and lecture to which Ridgeley escorted her, with Aunt Bess as her companion-chaperone.

Rumor had it that Ridgeley dipped rather deep at the gaming tables and, if he were not up the river tick, he was surely standing on its shores. Sarah dismissed such *on dits* as being of little concern, for they were simply none of her business—nor anyone else's so far as she could see, with the possible exception of the man's creditors.

Family dinners these days were not quite the same with both Matthew and Charles absent. Sarah, Emily, and Aunt Bess were glad to have the Brocktons with them. They helped dispel the gloom the others' absence left. Emily had been out the entire day as the family sat to dinner one evening.

"Was that not Hamilton Ridgeley leaving as I came in this afternoon? He seems to have an unusual interest in our household, would you not agree?" Emily asked with a great show of mischievous innocence.

Sarah gave her an exasperated look. "He was merely returning a book I loaned him last week."

"Does it appear to the rest of you that our Sarah has made a conquest?" Ever the tease, Emily was not about to give up such a topic. Precisely because they all knew Sarah's conduct had never been anything but thoroughly, even rigidly, proper, they entered into the fun and merriment of Emily's conversational gambit.

"Hmmm. As the only adult male in the household, I should hate to call the man out," Edward said, tongue firmly in cheek. "Just not good *ton* for a cleric, you know."

"Darling, no. You must not," his wife wailed in mock shock. "Think of our babies."

"Flowers and poetry and rides in the park. It is just too shocking." Aunt Bess assumed a self-righteous tone.

"For heaven's sake!" Sarah tossed her serviette on the table. Just when the others thought she had taken their teasing to heart and were about to apologize, her lips started to twitch and soon they were all laughing. "You really are too ridiculous, all of you. And truly you need not fear that my virtue is threatened by Hamilton Ridgeley—or anyone else for that matter."

"At least we have you laughing," Emily said.

"If you use that tactic again, young lady, I shall lock you in your chamber on bread and water for a week. And," she added darkly, "I shall think of some equally appropriate torture for the rest of you."

Social activities aside, Sarah pursued the establishment of a pottery on the Rosemont and Markholme properties. She secured the names of persons knowledgeable about the art and techniques of making pottery. However, none of these men—for they were, of course, all men—was interested in talking with a woman about their business. Sarah began to doubt she would be able to achieve her goal. Then she met Hector St. John Sinclair quite by accident. Later, Sarah was to declare that it was by Providence.

She and Emily had gone to Hookam's bookshop and lending library. As Emily browsed through the latest gothic novels, Sarah pored over art books. With a gasp of discovery, she plucked from the shelf a volume devoted to the making of pottery. A portly, middle-aged gentleman standing nearby observed her delight with keen appreciation. Having noted exactly which book she held, he watched her eagerly leaf through it, apparently oblivious to anything around her. After a time, he spoke.

"Pardon me, miss." He seemed aware of the impropriety of accosting a lady so. "Have you a particular interest in this subject?"

She turned to him in surprise. "Why, yes, I do. I had despaired of finding any detailed information. None of the men involved in this field seems at all interested speaking with a mere woman about it." This last came out with a trace of bitterness. "Oh, I beg your pardon."

"Perhaps you have not consulted the right ones," he said

amiably. "I happen to have knowledge of this field. Perhaps I can help you find what or whom you are seeking."

Sarah was aware that talking with a strange man was decidedly improper, but one did not ignore an opportunity when fate seemed to fling it in one's lap. She looked at him carefully. Dressed soberly and neatly, he had a round face, pink cheeks, and noticeable laugh lines around his clear blue eyes. When he inclined his head slightly, she saw that he sported a round bald spot like a tonsured monk.

"Oh? And you are . . . ?" She sounded just a bit haughty even to herself.

"Hector St. John Sinclair." He smiled and bowed.

"Oh!" She closed the book and looked again at the title and author on its spine. "This is your book! And I have heard of your work."

"That it is, miss."

"It is Madam," she said, extending her hand to him. "I am Lady Markholme. My husband is the Earl of Markholme. We—that is, I—have been considering the possibilities of establishing a pottery in Derbyshire, but Matthew is off with Wellington now and it is up to me and I have had a wretchedly difficult time getting anyone of consequence in this field to talk with me." Then she paused, embarrassed at pouring out her troubles in such a manner.

"I see," he said somewhat vaguely and somewhat amused.

"You worked with Josiah Wedgewood, I think."

"Yes," he said, surprised. "I left the firm these five years and more now. But retirement is not all it is reported to be. Thinking to keep my hand in somehow, I scratched out the volume you now hold."

"It looks to be quite thorough."

"I tried to include some of the history of the field—and compare our works with pottery from the East."

"You miss it, do you not?" she asked gently.

"Yes, I do. I still dabble at it in a small way in a back room. Drives Mrs. Sinclair mad at times. But it is not the same as what we were doing in the manufactory."

She bit her lip and looked at him thoughtfully. "Would you . . . would you be interested in getting involved in it again? Or could I possibly persuade you to come and discuss such a venture with me? I do so need advice from someone knowledgeable. . . ." Now she was being bold, indeed.

His eyes lit up. "I should be very happy to discuss such with you and I will happily call upon you at your convenience."

Sinclair was not only interested in getting involved in pottery again, he was eager to do so. He called the very next day and the two of them discussed her proposals at length. Then, armed with a letter to Mr. Howard, Sinclair set off for Derbyshire to study the possibilities for himself. A few days later, he once again settled himself in a comfortable chair in Lord Markholme's London library.

"I was not sure what I would find in Derbyshire, but I must say 'tis a fine idea you have there, my lady," he said with almost schoolboy eagerness. "The clay is of good quality and we will be able to build fine kilns, I am sure."

"Then you will join us?"

"I shall be glad to. Miriam—my wife, you know—says she would not mind moving back to the country." He chuckled. "Actually, she is happy I will not be underfoot all the time, though she allows a body with any sense would not be seeking hard work at my age."

Sarah smiled. "It is all settled then? We have an agreement?"

"Nearly so, my lady. There are one or two matters I should like to take up with you before we come to firm terms." He looked away thoughtfully and then brought his gaze back to hers. She waited expectantly.

It turned out that Mr. Sinclair, having worked with the Wedgewoods and being a follower of Robert Owen, was keenly interested in how Lord and Lady Markholme would provide for their workers. She assured him she and Matthew were prepared to accept the extra costs of adequate housing for employees and schooling for children.

"My husband and I feel that if you treat people properly, they will respond by working more productively. In the end, we all benefit. Do you not agree?"

"Most assuredly, my lady. And on that note, I am happy to offer my services."

Sarah bid him goodbye with a sense of subdued excitement. She would have much to write Matthew about tonight. Tomorrow, she would try to contact Mr. Samuel Whitbread about Matthew's brewery project.

# Seventeen

The footman sent as messenger to Mr. Whitbread returned with a note saying Mr. Whitbread had retired to his country estate a very ill man. This news left Sarah in a quandary, for Matthew had given her only the one name. Perhaps Adrian could advise her.

Adrian was a frequent visitor at Markholme House even after Matthew's departure. His connection with the War Office gave him access to news and details before they became public knowledge. In mid-April, as all England rejoiced at Napoleon's abdication and the somewhat anticlimactic news of Wellington's triumph at Toulouse, Adrian called to ask for a private word with Sarah.

"You have news of Matthew." It was a statement, not a question.

"Yes." Adrian took her hands in his. "He was wounded—but he is recovering."

"Where? How seriously?"

"A head wound and a gash in his leg. Hendley slipped me a note in the official dispatches. Matthew was unconscious for two or three days, but he is fine now. You must not worry, but I knew you would want to know."

"Yes. Thank you, Adrian."

"Coop will be coming home with him soon, I suspect."

"I hope so."

"He is going to be fine, Sarah. He has had good care,

I think. Hendley says he may limp a bit at first is all." He gave her hands a squeeze and released them.

"A limp I can live with." Sarah smiled nervously. "At least he is coming back to us."

"Yes. And we are going to need his help here now." Adrian wiped a hand across his face. "The Peninsular armies are to be disbanded. Wellington is opposed to that idea, but Parliament does not want the expense now that Boney is gone. They will all be coming home."

"To a country ill prepared for them." She had immediately perceived his worry.

"Right. Some will join the occupation forces in Belgium, but thousands will flood the countryside seeking jobs. Now that the war is ended with the United States, those troops will add to the lot."

She told him of Matthew's hope of establishing a brewery and was not surprised to learn her husband had already discussed the idea with his friend. When she mentioned her inability to consult Whitbread, Adrian patted her on the shoulder and said, "I will look into it."

Although the Betsworth ball the next evening was to be *the* social event of the season, Sarah seriously considered forgoing this pleasure. She knew Aunt Bess and Catherine would gladly accompany Emily, Edward having returned to the country. Emily and Catherine persuaded her to go with them arguing there was cause for celebration in the news that Matthew was likely on his way home.

Entering the Betsworths' spacious ballroom, they could see that the countess had achieved the dream of every London hostess—a veritable crush. Emily joined a group of young people and it was not long before she showed Sarah a filled dance card. Sarah's own dance card was not empty by any means, though she was glad to sit out several sets.

She had taken the floor with both Adrian and the Earl of Betsworth. Hamilton Ridgeley had also claimed her for a country dance during which they conversed pleasantly. She was mildly surprised when he insisted on a waltz later in the evening.

A few minutes afterward, she saw him on the sidelines in earnest discussion with Lady Poindexter and it appeared the two were not in charity with each other. Finally, he seemed to acquiesce to some demand of his cousin and with an ironic little bow, he walked away from her.

"I wonder what that was about?" Sarah asked herself, but mentally shrugged it off as none of her business.

When Ridgeley claimed his waltz, Sarah thought he was slightly tipsy, but he danced with his usual superior expertise, executing the steps with grace and control.

"You are looking gloriously beautiful this evening, my dear," he said, tightening his hold on her waist. Startled, she looked up at him and thought she saw a fleeting look of longing in his eyes, but it was gone so quickly she could not be sure.

"Why, thank you." She laughed nervously. "Any female appreciates a pretty compliment."

"But you are not just any female."

"Mr. Ridgeley!"

"Never mind, my dear," he murmured, drawing her a bit closer. "I know you are a proper married lady."

Nothing more was said as they whirled through the final steps of the dance, but neither did he loosen his hold on her. Returning to the sidelines, he drew her hand to his lips in a thank you. Such inordinate interest from a man thought to be merely a friend was disconcerting, but she attributed his behavior to too many trips to the punch bowl.

Later, as she sat talking with others, Sarah realized she had not seen Emily in a while. She glanced around, but did not see her. Suddenly, a footman appeared at her elbow and discreetly said, "Your sister has need of you, my lady. If you will just follow me . . ."

Slightly perplexed, Sarah followed him out of the ballroom and down a hallway. He paused, opened a door for her, and stepped back to allow her entrance.

The room was obviously the earl's library and, while it was not dark, it was less well lit than either the ballroom or the hallway had been. The room appeared empty.

"Emily?"

"She's not here, my dear." It was Hamilton Ridgeley's voice and his hand at her elbow as he stepped from behind the door and pushed it slightly to.

"Mr. Ridgeley?" she asked wonderingly.

"The same." He laughed, pulling her into his arms. "I had to see you alone, my love. I have long dreamed of having you in my arms."

"Mr. Ridgeley!" She addressed him as a governess would a small boy and pushed both hands against his chest. "You must be foxed. Now release me at once and let us return to the ballroom."

"Can't do that my darlin'." His words were faintly slurred. He tightened his arms around her and bent his head to capture her lips with his own. She struggled vainly and felt slightly suffocated in his tight embrace. He smelled of spirits. Then she heard voices at the door.

"Lady Markholme! Mr. Ridgeley!" The shocked tones came from none other than the straitlaced hostess of the evening.

Suddenly released from the vise of Ridgeley's arms, Sarah turned and saw several faces at the door, including those of her host and hostess; Lady Jersey; another, older gentleman; and—Lady Annalisa Poindexter.

"Well, I never . . . outrageous . . ." This pronouncement came from Lady Jersey who, as a patroness of Almack's, prided herself on being one of the arbiters of *ton* behavior. It flashed through Sarah's mind that Sally Jersey's nickname of "Silence" had not been earned by unwillingness to gossip.

"Hmph!" grunted the older man as the newcomers crowded into the room.

"I am sorry, my lady," Ridgeley said softly to Sarah. She thought the note of regret in his voice was genuine.

"I cannot believe you would embarrass the family this

way, Hamilton," Lady Poindexter said accusingly, but
Sarah thought her expression of outrage and chagrin did
not quite reach her eyes.

"You misunderstand. This is not what it seems at all."
Sarah tried to explain, but her words fell on deaf ears.

"We understand all too well, Lady Markholme," Annalisa said in a quietly contemptuous voice that carried
clearly. "Discretion, my dear. Discretion. One can get away
with most anything with discretion."

Instantly, Sarah knew that Annalisa had engineered this
little scene to achieve precisely the end it had produced—
profound embarrassment for the wife of Matthew
Cameron, Earl of Markholme. She looked from Ridgeley
to his cousin. In his eyes she saw shame and resignation;
in hers, disdain and triumph.

"If you will excuse me, I shall take my leave now." Sarah
addressed her statement to the earl and Countess of
Betsworth, and left the room, her head high.

She sent a footman to tell Aunt Bess she had taken ill,
retrieved her cloak, and had her carriage summoned.


Sarah ordered up a bath the instant she gained her own
bedchamber. Feeling soiled and used, she thought to
cleanse herself by soaking away the sordidness.

Still awake when the others returned—in fact, anticipat-
ing their arrival—she invited them into her sitting room
and told them everything. Emily said she, too, had been
called out of the ballroom on a spurious mission.

"Hamilton Ridgeley should be horsewhipped," Emily
sputtered.

"I quite agree, Emily," Sarah said calmly, "but I doubt
it would do much good. Lady Jersey and Lady Poindexter
will have the tale spread throughout the *ton* by noon tomorrow."

"Or sooner," Aunt Bess said. "It appears that Lady Poindexter has already been spreading a bit of poison linking
your name and her cousin's."

"But—but, there is simply nothing there," Sarah protested. "Until tonight, Mr. Ridgeley has always been all that is proper and I have never even been alone in his company. What could she possibly have to say?"

"That is just it, Sarah dear," Aunt Bess replied. "Nothing is actually said. Much is implied. This sort of wickedness achieves its purposes by innuendo and whisper."

"And it is extremely difficult to respond to," Catherine said. "An answer is seen as weakness, or, indeed, as admission. 'Where there is smoke, there must be fire,' and so on. Now—let us see how we can handle this broil."

"I was so looking forward to Matthew's return." The forlorn tone told the others more of her feelings for her husband than she might have intended. "Now, I cannot bear for him to hear of this."

"We cannot keep it from him," Catherine said pragmatically. "The first time he steps into White's he will hear of it. Men are much worse gossips than women, you know."

"I hope Matthew calls that blackguard Ridgeley out," Emily declared pugnaciously.

"Oh, no-o-o," Sarah wailed.

"We must try to forestall that happening." Catherine cast Emily a speaking look. "For the present, we must continue as if nothing untoward has occurred. We will go about our business as usual. I daresay your aunt's countenance means something in society. And I am sure Adrian will not desert us. It never hurts to have the heir to a dukedom on your side."

Sarah's spirits were bolstered by their support. Perhaps, she thought when they left, everything would turn out all right. Her own heretofore unsullied reputation would stand her in good stead. One married woman's indiscretion—fact or not—would be forgotten as soon as the next bit of salacious gossip started its rounds.

But would Matthew believe her innocent? Would he be outraged? Hurt? Cynical? Would he assume that she accepted society's view of marriages such as theirs—that such incidents, even when true, elicited only a wink and a snicker for those who were caught?

Whatever his reaction, she wondered if their fragile relationship could weather this onslaught. Oh, no doubt they could muddle through—indeed, they would have to—with one of those *ton* marriages in which the parties learned to tolerate each other.

But she had hoped for so much more. . . .

# Eighteen

Sarah's misgivings were well-founded. Matthew learned the latest London scandal upon his return to English soil.

The first available ship to carry wounded and demobilized troops landed in Plymouth, thus launching Matthew on a long, arduous land journey. With a hired coach and driver, he and Coop were on their way, accompanied by a Captain Wilson whom Matthew had met on board and offered transportation.

Eager for news of home, they devoured week-old newspapers at their first overnight stop. A gossip column caught Matthew's attention.

Despite her husband's soldierly sojourn with troops in France, Lady M. seems never to lack escort. We understand H.R. to be ever so attentive in that direction.

Lady M? H.R.? A soldier husband? Surely, not Sarah. But who else? Not Sarah, he told himself firmly. But memory taunted him. He had once before been profoundly mistaken about a woman. He could not put the item out of his mind.

Halfway through the journey, Matthew was sitting in the taproom of another inn, finishing a glass of port. They had arrived late to find the inn's only private parlor already occupied. Wanting only a meal and beds, he and Wilson had opted for the common rooms. Wilson and Coop had already retired when three fashionably dressed newcomers arrived, loudly demanding service and making raucous jokes.

Young and full of themselves, the three were eager to impress, dropping the names of notables in society and in the sporting world. Matthew was only half listening until they mentioned Emily. He smiled indulgently to hear her described as "the pick of the lot" on the marriage mart.

Then one said, "Her sister's quite a looker, too."

Another snorted derisively. "She's married. And older anyway."

"Don't seem to make any difference to Ridgeley. Saw him in the park with her once. Heard they was right cozy when old Betsworth caught 'em in his library," number one said with a leer in his voice.

No one noticed that the man at the next table had gone very still.

"I, for one, do not believe it," number three said firmly, earning Matthew's silent gratitude.

"Well, it's the truth, whether you want to believe it or not," one said pugnaciously.

"I think 'tis true," number two said, sounding reluctant. "M'mother said Lady Jersey was one of the ones caught 'em in a tight clinch."

" 'Silence' Jersey?" The doubtful one was sarcastic.

Keeping a bland expression, Matthew picked up his walking stick and pushed himself up from his chair. He was surprised at the ease with which a pillar of stone could negotiate stairs.

Sleep eluded him.

At dawn, his bed resembled a ship tossed mercilessly by a storm. Hearing the major stumble clumsily, Coop rose instantly from his cot to resurrect the fire.

"Never mind that, Coop," Matthew growled. "Let us have some breakfast and be on the road. Rouse Wilson, will you? And order up the coach."

The innkeeper mumbled about gentry blokes that kept
a man up all night and then wanted their breakfast at the
crack of dawn, but he happily accepted a bit extra on the
bill. Matthew ate little. In the coach, his leg propped on
the opposite seat, he feigned sleep to avoid conversation
with his two companions.

No matter how he tried to consider other things, the
conversation of the night before haunted him. He knew
who Ridgeley was. He had known the man casually as Annalisa's favorite relative when they were all a good deal
younger. Ridgeley, a man-about-town, popular in sporting
circles, was known to have a way with the ladies. H.R. It
was no surprise Sarah should have met the man, but why
was it such a shock that she had succumbed to his charms?
For surely, she had. That item in the paper hinted at such.
Sally Jersey loved gossip, but she was not known to spread
untruths.

Matthew did not relish being the cuckolded husband in
the sordid little drama his imagination laid out for him.
The very thought of another man touching Sarah infuriated him. And she had apparently allowed it! Had Ridgeley
been able to elicit the passion she shared with her husband? No man, having sampled that, would be able to leave
her alone.

He groaned inwardly. Only he must have done so aloud,
too, for Coop said, "Is the leg a'painin' ye, my lord?"

"I am all right." Matthew shifted about on the seat.

Good God! How could he have been such a fool as to
trust a woman again? Thank all the powers that be, he had
not allowed himself to fall in love with her. To have endured such humiliation once was insupportable; twice was
beyond enough.

His mood darkened as the day wore on. When they
stopped to change horses and have lunch, Matthew ate
very little, though he ordered not one, but two tankards
of strong ale. He dozed off and on as the journey resumed.

In midafternoon the carriage passed a long row of lilac

bushes still in bloom along the roadside. Their smell wafted through the sun-warmed air.

Matthew woke with a start, momentarily disoriented.

"Sarah?" he murmured. Then he was fully awake. Instantly he recognized the familiar scent and recalled his sense of betrayal. A gut-wrenching pain slowly dissolved to a dull, persistent ache.

That night Matthew made no pretense of joining Wilson for the evening meal. He ordered up a bottle of brandy and sought the solitude of his own chamber. The next morning, he appeared to be himself again.

The next day they reached London.


The days following the Betsworth ball were among the most miserable of Sarah's life. Most of her misery came as she anticipated Matthew's return.

There was no noticeable decline in callers at Markholme House, though Sarah was sure certain of them came merely to satisfy their curiosity. Catherine insisted that she and Sarah call upon some of the *ton's* most elevated persons. None of their prospective hostesses returned a "not at home" message, though Sarah found the conversations rather strained at times.

There was one very uncomfortable moment when Sarah and Catherine called upon the dowager Duchess of Islington to find Lady Poindexter among the guests.

"I was so proud of you," Catherine said later as they were seated in their carriage. "Your 'Lady Poindexter' and that cool little nod were exactly right. She hardly knew how to react."

"Thank you. You were pretty wonderful yourself diverting the conversation to Princess Caroline's latest escapade."

"It helped that Adrian was there. I knew we could count on him to see that no whisper of scandal would discredit Matthew's bride."

Apprised of the entire situation, Adrian had been quick

to rally to his friends' defense. His presence in the Duchess's drawing room indicated his support, for Sarah knew he ordinarily eschewed such affairs. Finding Ridgeley's behavior both despicable and perplexing, Adrian promised to do what he could to quell gossip in the gentlemen's clubs. Sarah knew "what he could do" would be considerable.

Nevertheless, she knew they were trying to limit the damage of a fire already out of control. If Sarah harbored doubts about the stir the gossip caused in London drawing rooms, they were dispelled by that nasty little item in *The Morning Post.*

Besides restoring—or maintaining—her own credit with society, Sarah was still occupied with projects of renovation in the London house and plans for Markholme Hall and the pottery in Derbyshire. She had written Matthew, but he, of course, had not had time to consider and respond to her suggestions—assuming he received her messages. Now Matthew would be home soon.

Adrian reported that Samuel Whitbread was on his deathbed, effectively closing that avenue for carrying out Matthew's brewery plans. So far Adrian had been unable to find another brewer to consult. Sarah felt a keen sense of defeat and disappointment. She had failed Matthew in the one task he had asked of her. She was still not wholly convinced of the advisability of establishing a brewery, but she honestly intended to support Matthew in this project.

Uncertain when Matthew would arrive, Sarah busied herself in the library from which she could hear the front door knocker. She would hold her breath, waiting to hear a familiar deep voice, but for two days she had been repeatedly disappointed. She began to fear he had had a carriage accident, or fallen ill, or been waylaid by highwaymen, or . . .

The entire family, including Edward, who had come in from the country only the day before, and the children, who were being allowed a special treat in joining the grown-ups, gathered in the drawing room for tea. Like the rest of the house, this room—in green, gold, and ecru—had been recently redecorated.

Everyone seemed to be talking at once as Emily played the pianoforte softly. Sarah was seated with her back to the door and three-year-old Katie-Ann leaned on her knee, earnestly telling her a story about her doll who had also been allowed to come to tea. Suddenly, the rest of the room went quiet. Sarah looked up to see them all staring at the door. Turning that way herself, she saw him.

"Matthew!" three of them cried at once.

He stood in the doorway, looking thinner than she remembered and leaning heavily on his walking stick. His gaze took in the utter domesticity of the scene and it flashed across his mind this was what made a soldier's hardships worthwhile. Then he caught himself—if only it were real. He seemed frozen as he watched his wife rise and come toward him. She put her arms around him and hugged him close. Lilac again. He hesitated a mere fraction of a second before returning her embrace with the arm not supporting himself on the walking stick.

"Welcome home, my darling," she murmured for his ears alone.

She looked up at him, her gaze lingering briefly on his lips. She wanted to kiss him, but mindful of their audience and having sensed his hesitation, she restrained herself. Her eyes met his, and something in his gaze told her it was just as well she had not. She slowly withdrew and turned.

Then he was showered with the warm affection of his sister and cheerful greetings from the rest.

"Here. Sit here," Edward said, having risen from a chair near the tea table. Matthew took the proffered seat and there was a moment of silence.

Katie-Ann sidled up to him. "Uncle Matthew, is your leg hurted?" she asked sympathetically.

"Yes, moppet, it is, but it will be better soon, I think." He touched her curls and then pulled her onto his other knee. "But the other one still works as a seat for a pretty little girl." She giggled and draped an arm around his neck.

This much is real anyway, he thought.

Sarah had rung for fresh tea and now busied herself preparing a plate for him, pouring tea for him, and replenishing the others' cups. She then took a seat and contented herself just looking her fill at him while the others talked.

"Is the wound very painful, my dear?" Aunt Bess asked.

"Not anymore. Fatiguing more than painful."

"The scar above your eye will probably fade with time," Catherine offered. "It does add rather a rakish look, I think. My brother, the pirate."

He pretended to take offense. "Not 'My brother, the brave soldier home from war' or 'My brother, hero extraordinaire'—oh, no. She must make me out a pirate."

"We cannot allow you to get too top-lofty." Catherine grinned at him.

"I have no fear of that." His voice was rich with irony.

"I suppose you've heard of Wellington's elevation," Edward said.

"Yes. We saw a recent newspaper and met several people along the way who managed to fill us in with all the news." Matthew looked involuntarily at his wife and she instinctively knew it was not only news of Wellington that he had heard.

Sarah listened to the ensuing conversation about government plans for a great victory celebration. However, her mind was awhirl with the fact that Matthew had heard of the incident in the Betsworth library. What had he heard? And from whom? And, most importantly, how much of what he had heard did he believe? Her heart ached at having him so near but untouchable.

Her attention was diverted by young Ned who came to stand quietly by his uncle's chair. He waited as stoically as any boy of five could until there was a lull in conversation. He plucked Matthew's sleeve and almost whispered, "Did you kill him, Uncle Matthew?"

"Did I kill . . . ?" Matthew asked, puzzled.

"Did you kill the Frenchy what wounded you?" the boy repeated patiently.

Matthew smiled at him and drew him in with the arm not holding his sister. "Well, now . . . no, I did not. At the risk of destroying your image of Uncle Matthew, the hero, I must tell you I never saw the man. You see, he shot my horse, and when that happened, I fell and that was that."

"I bet you would have if you could, though," Ned said loyally.

"I probably would have tried." Matthew hugged the boy to him briefly.

"I think we had better let Uncle Matthew get some rest now," Catherine said, ushering the children out.

Soon the others took themselves off to attend errands, real or manufactured to allow Matthew and Sarah time alone.

"Are you very tired then, Matthew?" Sarah asked after an awkward pause.

"Not exceedingly. I am glad to be rid of that coach, however."

"I am sure you are. It was a long journey and a hired coach is rarely comfortable. You had good weather, though."

"Yes." He looked at her directly. His eyes seemed to ask if they were going to skirt around the subject uppermost in both their minds. But he said nothing.

Sarah lowered her gaze and sighed inaudibly. She did not know how to introduce the subject. He seemed so cool and indifferent. She was confused and fearful. But the fear had become entangled with angry resentment, too. How dare he judge her without hearing her side of things? Well, she could be just as cool and indifferent at he!

"Our renovations are proceeding apace," she offered with a gesture at the room around them. "I think this room turned out nicely."

"Indeed. You have done well, Sarah."

Encouraged, she asked, "Would you like to see the plans for the Hall? And the pottery?"

"Yes, I would. Are they in the library?"

"Yes. I will get them." She started for the door.

"No. That will not be necessary." His tone was harsher than he intended and he tempered it. "I am not an invalid. I need practice negotiating stairs."

At the bottom of the stairs, she watched him come down one laborious step at a time, his injured leg stiff and awkward. She could see sweat on his upper lip and hear his strained breathing by the time he reached the bottom.

"Coming down is harder than going up," he said.

She seated him at the big desk and stood at his elbow as he perused the plans she laid before him. She explained that they would modernize the kitchen and enlarge the library at Markholme Hall. At one point, when she reached to bring another sheet into view, her hand brushed against his. Each of them quickly withdrew from the touch.

He flipped the pages over silently, studying them carefully. Then he started through them again. When he had finished, he looked up at her. Their eyes locked for a moment, then he turned back to the plans and cleared his throat.

"I like it," he said. For the first time since he had stood in the doorway earlier, she felt a trace of his old warmth toward her. "May I see the plans for the upper floors again?"

He studied these sheets closely.

"What is this?" he asked, indicating a suite of rooms in the east wing. "Surely we do not need yet another elaborate guest chamber."

"No," she said slowly. "It is . . . well, I thought to make those rooms the nursery . . . and schoolrooms. I thought it would be more convenient to have these rooms on the same floor as our . . . as other family bedchambers." She could feel herself blushing and hated doing so. "But if you object . . ."

"No, no. They seem to be far enough removed from

guest chambers to pose no problem. Are you sure you want them so near our—uh, your—own rooms?"

"Why, yes." Her surprise was evident. "That was, after all, the whole point of moving those rooms. But if you had rather not . . ."

"No, no. I have no objection." He quickly flipped to another sheet. "The servants' quarters seem vastly improved. And larger."

"I thought to leave room for growth," she said defensively.

"I did not intend the comment as criticism, Sarah." He turned to look up at her.

"Oh."

"Now, please pull up that chair over there and tell me about this pottery business."

# Nineteen

Sarah barely finished telling Matthew about the pottery by the time to dress for dinner. They had not discussed his brewery plans, nor had either of them broached the more personal subject uppermost in their minds. Each of them thought the other deliberately skirted that issue.

We will get to it later, I suppose, Sarah thought.

Despite its requiring him to negotiate stairs at least three more times that day, Matthew chose to sit with the family rather than dine in his chamber. Overall, dinner was a pleasant affair. Edward and Matthew did not linger over their port, and a convivial family group gathered in the drawing room later. If others sensed any tension, they were careful to conceal their concerns.

As she prepared for bed, Sarah wondered whether Matthew would come to her that night. She had dismissed the maid and was about to climb into bed with a book when there was a rap on the dressing room door and he entered, clearly prepared for bed himself. He leaned heavily on the walking stick.

"I just came to wish you a good night," he said. There was a brief pause. "This is not the way I had planned my homecoming, but under the circumstances"—he patted his wounded leg—"perhaps it would be better if we slept apart."

"As you wish, Matthew." Did he expect her to beg him to share her bed?

"Sarah?" He moved a little closer, allowing her to catch the familiar scent that was his alone.

She was nearly undone by it and was surprised she was able to keep from flinging herself at him. Her eyes held an unasked question.

"Best to remove myself from temptation. You do understand?" he asked, not ungently. He lifted her chin and bent to kiss her on the forehead.

"Yes, I think I do." She twisted away abruptly, unable to suppress the tone of resignation and bitterness. "You must make sure any issue of this marriage is yours. And the only way to do that is to stay away from me until you know for sure I am not carrying someone else's bastard. Is that not so? Well, you should not have to wait more than a week or two, my lord."

"Sarah!" He was taken aback by her bluntness. "That is not what I intended at all."

"Is it not?" She rounded on him. "If you will but remember, my dear sir, we have in the past occasionally been able to sleep in the same bed without—how did Shakespeare put it?—ah, yes, making the beast with two backs."

"There is no need to be crude about it, my dear." He sounded rather pompous and haughty.

"I see—I am crude in speaking bluntly. But what are you—you who assume your wife has been whoring around? You cannot bring yourself to speak of a rumor you heard from strangers, but you are perfectly ready to take it for truth, are you not?"

"Now who is making assumptions?"

"Matthew, you cannot even bring yourself to kiss me properly. You were not so cold when we parted in Portsmouth a few weeks ago."

"Is that our problem here?" he asked, losing whatever control he had maintained. "We can remedy that without much difficulty!"

He dropped his cane and pulled her roughly into his arms, assaulting her lips with his. She pushed against his chest and tried to twist her face away, but he grabbed her head and held it as he kissed her, his lips hard and insistent. He thrust his tongue against her closed lips, daring her to open to him. With a sob in her throat, she did so, and she was kissing him back with the same vigor and anger and passion he leveled at her. Finally, he thrust her from him. He was breathing hard.

"There. Was that satisfactory? Is that how he kissed you? More to the point—is that how you responded to him?"

"How dare you?" She was seething now. "How dare you condemn me out of hand on the basis of some bit of idle gossip?" She pulled her arm back to deliver a hard slap.

"I dare all right." He grabbed her wrist in mid-stroke. "I do not hear you denying you were caught with Ridge-ley kissing you. But I do insist you play by my rules, dear wife. You may spread your favors as you will—*after* we have got my heir." He bent to pick up his cane.

She marched over to the dressing room door and held it open. "I bid you good night, my lord." She refused to look at him.

Matthew lay awake cursing himself. He should have confronted her about Ridgeley to begin with—just get it out in the open and go on from there. What other choice did they have? The marriage had to continue on some basis. Financial considerations aside, there were all those other people dependent on the two of them.

Sarah was wrong in thinking his concern about an heir the reason for his reluctance to make love to her. God! How he wanted to do so. Any discomfort would have been small price to pay. He had wanted her all day. He wanted her right now. But ugly pictures kept intruding: another man kissing her, holding her, intimately caressing her, and—worse—her returning such caresses. These images had haunted him for days now. Seeing her, touching her, smelling her light perfume had intensified the pain.

The irony of this situation struck him. Had not another Matthew Cameron, Earl of Markholme, been brought low by a Rosemont woman? Like mother, like daughter? Well, he was damned if any woman would bring him to utter ruin. One had tried before—and nearly succeeded. But he had been in love before. His pain then was understandable. This time, by God, love had no role at all.

Come now, Cameron. What a bounder. When did any other woman, even your precious boyhood love, ever stir you as this one does? And what other woman ever—ever— responded as sweetly and as enthusiastically as Sarah?

But who is to say she does not respond equally well to another?

Do you?

No.

Then why assume she does?

She is a woman—her mother's daughter.

She is a human being. Do you truly believe each human being responds to every other human being in the same way?

Of course not. What a beef-witted idea.

But that is precisely the assumption on which you base all this jealousy, is it not?

Jealousy? *Jealousy?*

Yes, you dolt. Jealousy. You know. The green-eyed monster and all that?

Jealousy presupposes strong attachment—at least a tendre for the damsel.

Ye-e-ss?

All right. Maybe I am a bit overly possessive. She is my wife, after all. But I am not in love with her. I will never be in love again.

Have it your way, Cameron. . . . For now.


The next day Matthew was just finishing his breakfast when Sara came down. Dark circles under her eyes gave him pause. A footman brought in fresh coffee.

"At your convenience, my lady, I should like a word with you. I shall be in the library."

She nodded.

As she entered the library, he had the plans for the pottery spread out before him. He stood as she entered to take a seat in front of the desk.

"Yes, my lord?"

"Please, Sarah do stop 'my lording' me," he said impatiently as he sat down again.

"As you wish." Her voice was coolly indifferent.

"I want to apologize for my behavior last night." He tried to catch her eye.

"Your behavior?" She stared above his head.

"Yes. I am sorry I was so rough with you."

She looked at him questioningly.

"When I kissed you."

"You are sorry you kissed me."

"No. I am not sorry I kissed you." He placed his hands flat on the desk and leaned toward her.

"You just said you were."

"I said I regretted being so rough."

"Will that be all, my lord—uh, Matthew?"

"Yes . . . no. I have a few questions about this pottery business. And I should like to know if you were able to get the information I needed on a brewery."

"No, I was not." She explained briefly about Samuel Whitbread's being unavailable.

"Did you seek information from anyone else?"

"You gave me only Mr. Whitbread's name." She sounded defensive.

"But you were able to find and even form some sort of alliance with a stranger in the business of making pottery, were you not?"

"Yes, but I told you that came about quite by accident."

"A fortuitous accident, it seems. Tell me, wife, did you think to put me off the notion of a brewery? You were never enthusiastic about this idea."

"No! That was not my intent at all. I do have reservations about a brewery, but I have done nothing to try to put obstacles in your way."

" 'Nothing' about sums it up."

She did not respond to this statement.

He continued, "However, things seem to be perfectly in order with the pottery. If you were waiting for my approval, you shall have it." He knew he sounded grudging. He wanted to elaborate, to tell her the plans were excellent, that he was especially pleased their workers would be better cared for than was usually the case. But he could not bring himself to do so in the face of her indifference this morning.

"Thank you," she said tonelessly. "Now, if you will excuse me—"

He lifted a hand in a small, resigned gesture as she rose and left the room.

The next weeks were chilly in the Markholme household as Matthew and Sarah did little to pull down the wall between them. He sought activities taking him away from home. She filled her days as she had prior to his return.

They were civil to each other. They even attended some social affairs together, but they invariably rode with others, and once at a function, each sought the company of a separate group of friends. When his injury finally allowed him to dance, he would seek her for a country dance or a quadrille, but never for a waltz which would, perforce, have put her in his arms for an extended period. She took little comfort from the fact that he danced with no one else. Both participated politely in conversations at dinner or over tea, but they directed few questions or comments specifically to each other. They handled estate matters in a businesslike manner with minimal discussion.

Their estrangement was not lost on others. Catherine and Aunt Bess often exchanged despairing looks and privately plotted to end this impasse. One evening, these two finally found the opportunity they had been seeking.

Lord and Lady Markholme, along with her aunt and his sister, were to attend a musicale. Lady Hambdon had managed a social coup in obtaining Signora Francosi as the principal entertainment of the evening. Before the performance, guests were free to mingle and partake of refreshments. As usual these days, Matthew excused himself and crossed the room to join another conversation.

Presently the three women of his own party observed that Annalisa Poindexter had not only joined Matthew's group, but stood next to him. She appeared to flirt with him, looking at him laughingly and often touching his arm.

"Drat that woman," Aunt Bess whispered to Catherine as Sarah's attention was diverted.

"Drat that man!" Catherine replied.

"What if he sits with her? Do we carry out our plan?"

"Yes. I shall see that he sits with us. You just work on your part."

Across the room, Matthew had, along with the others, politely accepted Lady Poindexter in their group. After some meaningless, flirtatious chitchat, she murmured, "Stroll with me a moment, Matthew."

He looked at her inquiringly, hesitated, then offered her his arm.

"I want to tell you how sorry I am about that little contretemps at the Betsworth ball." She kept her voice low.

"Little contretemps?" His voice was carefully neutral.

"Well, all right. Perhaps a bit more than that." She gave a small, artificial laugh. "I had no idea Hamilton was so . . . so . . . enamored. . . ." Her voice trailed off on a regretful note. When Matthew merely looked at her, she went on, "Or that the two of them would so lose themselves to propriety."

He stopped midstep and faced her squarely. "I told you before I do not discuss my wife, my lady," he said coldly. "That includes any nasty bit of gossip motivated by spite and malice."

"Let us not draw attention." A placating note in her voice, she tugged at his arm slightly. "I was merely offering apologies for any discomfort the gossip may be causing. After all, Hamilton is related to me and I am well aware of the devastating effect he has on women. I did not mean to upset you."

"You did not upset me."

"In any event, such an incident will not occur again. Temptation has been removed. Hamilton has departed our fair shores for an extended tour of the continent."

Matthew did not respond. Annalisa did not seem to notice the iron rigidity of his jaw. After an awkward bit of silence, she shrugged and said something about Signora Francosi's being the latest sensation of the opera world.

When he returned her to the group they had left, his sister approached to claim him just as the hostess announced the beginning of the program. Matthew was puzzled by Catherine's behavior, but there was no time to question it.

The singer was quite good and held her audience well. However, Matthew noticed Aunt Bess seemed a little pale, and she often touched her handkerchief to her mouth.

During the interval, she said, "Oh, my. I am not feeling very well at all. If you will excuse me, I shall return home."

"I am so sorry," Catherine said. "You are not looking well, either, my dear. Shall I accompany you?"

"If you please," Aunt Bess said weakly.

"We shall all come with you," Matthew said.

"Of course," Sarah concurred.

"Oh, no. Please. I know how much you have looked forward to this event, Sarah, dear. I am sure this is nothing serious. A bit of an indisposition only. I should feel so much worse were I to ruin your evening, too." She included Matthew in her apologetic look.

Some mild arguing convinced the couple to stay and enjoy the rest of the program. Once the carriage door was closed and the vehicle under way, Catherine and Aunt Bess turned to each other and broke into a peal of girlish giggles.

"You were magnificent," Catherine said. "That rice powder was just the right touch."

"I think we pulled it off," Aunt Bess crowed. "Now if

those two stubborn hard heads will just seize the opportunity we have forced upon them."

As Matthew and Sarah prepared to depart the Hambdon residence, Lady Poindexter's party was also in the entrance awaiting a carriage. Sarah had successfully avoided the woman all evening.

A footman brought Sarah's evening wrap and Matthew placed it around his wife, allowing his hands to rest momentarily on her shoulders. She looked up at him, her eyes reflecting the reaction his touch always brought, but she quickly recovered herself.

Matthew had instinctively thought to shield her from the spite and malice he had mentioned to Annalisa. It was one thing for him to be unhappy with her behavior, but it was quite another thing entirely for anyone else to presume something untoward in her actions.

He knew the gossip about his wife, but tonight was the first time anyone, aside from Adrian, had spoken of it to him directly. Adrian held the view that Sarah was wholly innocent, though he was unable to explain Ridgeley's behavior. But then Adrian was inordinately fond of Sarah. The rage Matthew felt tonight was not directed at Sarah, but at those who sought to besmirch her character.

For some days now he had been trying to find a way to lessen the tension between himself and his wife. As they settled into the carriage, he deliberately sat closer to her than necessary. She held herself stiffly away from him.

Matthew's mouth was disturbingly close to her ear as he asked, "Do you think we might put this unpleasantness behind us?"

"Just pretend it never happened?"

"Whatever happened is in the past." He thought himself very magnanimous in forgiving her. "We need to get on with the real purposes of this marriage."

"Which are?"

"You know as well as I do that a great many people

depend on us for their livelihood and well-being. We need to return to the working partnership we had before I left for France."

"Are you dissatisfied with any of the decisions I made in your absence?" Her voice had that carefully neutral tone she used with him lately.

"No, of course not. Have I not approved every single plan you have laid before me?"

"Well, then, I do not understand . . ."

He sighed impatiently. "All right, I'll be blunt—I want you back in my bed. Or, me in yours," he added in a lighter tone.

"To get an heir."

"Yes."

"Because that is a condition of our bargain."

"In part." He slid his arm across the back of the seat and leaned closer, his voice low. "But I also want you. I need you, Sarah. Can you honestly say you do not want me, too?"

He nuzzled her neck, kissing the sensitive area just below her ear and trailing light little kisses over her face. She did not resist. In fact, as his lips found hers, she put up a hand to caress his cheek and jaw. The kiss was a gentle, sweet, insistent—and full of promise.

"Can you?" he asked softly.

"Can I what?" Her voice now had a dreamy quality.

He chuckled softly. "Can you honestly say you do not want me, too?"

"No. I mean, yes. I do want you, too." She turned to put her arms around his neck. "I have missed you, Matthew."

"Me, too, sweetheart." His voice was husky and his lips urgent as he pulled her tighter to him.

Neither of them had quite recovered—nor did either want to—when the carriage arrived at their door.

# Twenty

Sarah awakened later than usual the next morning. She yawned, stretched luxuriously, rang for her maid, and snuggled back into the bedding to savor the night.

Betsy arrived shortly. As she came fully into the room, the maid was obviously—and none too successfully—holding back amused merriment. Sarah looked at her questioningly, and then turned a bright red as she observed the room strewn with various articles of her clothing and Matthew's.

Their lovemaking had lost none of its intensity, energy, or gentleness. Sarah smiled. More intensity and energy than gentleness the first time, she thought. Then, by tacit agreement, they had deliberately slowed the pace to explore and relearn, to prolong the exquisite pleasure of their too-long postponed reunion.

Still, something was missing. They had not achieved the oneness of spirit she remembered. Nor had Matthew stayed the night with her. She had fallen asleep in his arms, but sometime later she sensed he had gone. She waited and when he did not return, she felt slightly bereft.

Enough, she told herself. Swinging her legs out of bed and quickly instructing Betsy on wardrobe items, she arose to face the day.

* * *

In June the *ton* left no stone unturned in celebrating England's triumph over the Corsican upstart who had so overreached himself in trying to dominate Europe. The grandest of the festivities was an elaborate ball at Carlton House hosted by the Prince Regent.

Sarah knew she and Matthew were in good looks that evening, he in his regimentals and she in midnight blue silk which made her eyes appear darker than usual. She noted with some surprise and a great deal of pride that both the Prince and the guest of honor, Wellington, held up the reception line to lavish praise on her husband.

"I see you have recovered from that mishap at Toulouse," Wellington said as he clasped Matthew's hand. "Is it true you intend to sell out, Major?"

"Yes, sir, it is. It is time I turned to domestic duties."

"I certainly understand those concerns," the duke replied, "but I regret losing a good man."

"Thank you, sir. I like to think I may be of some use to fellows coming home now."

"No doubt you will." Wellington greeted Sarah politely, and then she and Matthew were quite literally pushed through the rest of the reception line.

"You did not tell me you were selling out."

"I assumed you knew. I returned to the Peninsula only because I gave him—the duke, I mean—my word to do so."

It was true. They had discussed this possibility early in their relationship. That it had not been a topic in recent weeks was yet another indication of the distance still separating them.

Demobilization of the Peninsular armies brought Richard Hendley, newly promoted to the rank of captain, to a post near London. One of the army's newest lieutenants, Charles Longbourne, would undergo additional training with a local militia before eventually joining the army of occupation in Belgium. For Emily, this meant that her two favorite soldiers would be able to attend her ball in early July.

Despite her modest expectations, Emily was one of the season's preeminent debutantes. Prior to Matthew's return, a young baronet had approached Sarah for permission to address the irrepressible Emily. To her credit, Emily refused the young man's proposal, but kept his friendship.

Thereafter, Sarah made it a point to see whether Emily favored a particular young man. Outgoing and friendly, she treated them all alike. Even when Hendley reappeared on the London scene, Emily did not focus her attention on any one suitor. It was true, though—and a source of some concern to Sarah—that if Emily granted more than one dance of an evening to anyone, it would be to the captain.

Emily sought her sister in Sarah's chamber one afternoon.

"Sarah, may I talk with you about something important?"

"Of course, dear. I was just sorting through some of these old garments. Come, sit for a while."

"You know," Emily said, taking a seat and twisting her hands in her lap, "I refused Sir Geoffrey's offer. Last night I discouraged Viscount Worthington from seeking to approach Matthew. And . . . there have been others who might have done so, had I encouraged them at all."

"I have noticed you never want for a dance partner."

"It is very gratifying to have so much attention. And I am having a wonderful time at balls and routs . . ."

"But?"

"But I am wondering if it is truly necessary that I find a suitable *parti* this season? In fact, is it absolutely necessary that I marry at all?"

"You are not interested in marrying?"

"I cannot like the thought of marrying where my affections are not engaged. I—I know that you and Matthew—" Her voice trailed off and color flooded Emily's cheeks as she looked at Sarah.

Sarah considered her sister silently for a moment, then

ignored the reference to her own marriage. "You need not choose a suitor who does not appeal to you. But you must know life as a maiden lady is quite untenable."

"I cannot believe it worse than marrying someone one has little regard for. Especially if one's affections are engaged elsewhere."

"And are your affections engaged?" Sarah asked gently.

"I—I think so."

"Has this young man made you an offer?"

"No. He would never be so improper as to offer for me without first consulting my guardian." Emily sounded impatient with such a refined sense of propriety. "I am not sure he even cares for me. And his prospects are not good."

"I see," Sarah said, knowing that she did see—all too well. "There will be a marriage portion for you, Emily, but not an overly generous one. It truly would be best if you could attach one of the more eligible young men."

"And if I cannot?"

Sarah's heart sank. "Your marriage portion could add a modest *supplement* to other income if one were frugal."

"And if one could persuade another to accept it," Emily said in a forlorn little voice.

"You have plenty of time, my dear." Sarah patted her sister's shoulder. "Who knows? Perhaps you will find your interest fixed in another direction—if not this year, next year, or the year after. Time or fate—or whatever—does seem to have a way of working things out for us."

"But I do not want to wait for time or whatever," Emily said with the impatience of youth immemorial. "And I doubt my interest will ever be diverted elsewhere."

"I understand, love. Truly, I do. Were I a fairy godmother, I would wave my magic wand for you. But none of us can dictate the affections of others. Indeed, we cannot even dictate our own, I fear."

Emily looked up at the sadness in her sister's voice.

"I'm sorry, Sarah. I did not mean to burden you with my problems. I do thank you for being patient with me and for allowing me such time as I may require."

\* \* \*

The conversation with Emily troubled Sarah. She had hoped for, worked for, an advantageous match for her sister. Her disappointment carried a degree of resentment, though she thought she had successfully hidden that. After all, had Sarah not subjected herself to a marriage of convenience in part to secure the best possible chance for Emily? Now Emily would just toss aside that chance? On the other hand, she recognized the heartache beneath the gaiety Emily showed others. Also, she was honest enough to admit that, for her, the marriage was, at the very least, agreeable. Still, Sarah wished she could do something to ease Emily's pain.

Emily turned to music to help work out her problems. Sarah turned to the soil.

Thus, one afternoon Sarah was on her knees, digging energetically and chastising herself anew for allowing weeds to get the better of her. At the far end of the garden, she was effectively hidden by some tall shrubs.

She did not mean to eavesdrop when Matthew and Richard Hendley came out to take a turn about the garden. As they approached a bench on the other side of her shrubbery, Richard was telling Matthew a rather risqué story of an event in Toulouse after Matthew left. Sarah knew the young man would be embarrassed to know she had overheard this conversation. To spare him any discomfort, she stayed put. She was trapped, but later she and Matthew would have a good laugh over her predicament.

The two men sat in what appeared to be companionable silence for a moment or two.

"What happened to Jamison?" Hendley asked. "I have not seen him since Toulouse."

"Probably still down in Kent. He is to be married. The vicar's daughter finally agreed to have him."

"Is he selling out?"

"No. Plans to have his bride join him in Belgium."

"You disapprove?"

"Not my place to approve or disapprove. But a country vicar's daughter following the drum?"

"I see your point." Hendley hesitated fractionally. "But half of English society seems to be making plans to go to Belgium or Paris now that the war is over."

"I wonder if it truly is over?" Matthew mused. "Bonaparte may be exiled to an island, but he still has followers in the French army."

"You think the vicar's daughter may be in danger even in Belgium?"

"Belgium aside, following the drum is no life for a gently bred female—particularly a very young woman." Matthew was adamant. "It is too hard on the woman and she usually distracts her husband from his duties."

"You may be right." Hendley did not sound convinced. "My mother managed well enough, but then she came from a military family."

"Remember Webster's wife in Portugal? Poor girl cried for months, she was so homesick and unhappy. And Webster was practically useless until he sent her home."

"True. Belgium is not the Peninsula, though."

There was another period of silence. Then Hendley changed the subject.

"I know you had little choice in the matter—given the title and all—but are you sorry about selling out?"

On the other side of the shrubbery, Sarah held her breath for Matthew's answer. He spoke slowly.

"Not exactly. It was time to move on. I knew my life would change when I accepted the terms of my inheritance."

"But you do have regrets."

"Yes. Of course. The army was my life for nearly twelve years. Why? Are you thinking of selling out?"

"No. Good lord, no. Even if—uh, the girl—would have me, I could not just sell out. I have no other visible, or invisible, means of supporting myself, let alone a wife."

"*The* girl?"

"Any girl. Anyone. It was just an idle thought." Sarah could hear the embarrassment in Hendley's response.

"Just as well," Matthew said and Sarah imagined him patting the younger man's shoulder. "Most of the ladies on the marriage mart aim for advantageous matches."

"Like Emily."

"Yes. Like Emily. Oh, she will have a marriage portion. A very modest one. But she needs a title and wealth to maintain any sort of position in society."

"She has looks and charm. She should have little difficulty achieving that goal."

"None at all."

"I wish her well." Hendley sounded sincere.

"You know," Matthew said thoughtfully, "it is not quite true that you would have no other means of support. You know how to lead men and manage materials. Those are skills useful in civilian life, too."

"I could never give up the army! 'Tis in my blood. Family heritage and all that, don't you know? His Majesty's Forces can count on me for some time yet."

Their discussion shifted to the merits of horses they had inspected at Tattersall's earlier and soon they rose and strolled back into the house.

Sarah remained sitting on her feet. Did her husband's generally low opinion of women extend to his wife? It must. After all, they had known each other for only a few months.

He had discouraged the captain from thinking of marrying. Sarah could only be glad of that, for the not-fully-acknowledged recipient of the captain's attention appeared to be her sister. Such a match was simply not one to be encouraged. In time Emily would surely settle on a more eligible member of her court of admirers.

To what degree did Matthew regret his own marriage? Had he not been forced into marrying, he might have turned the management of his property over to a steward and a solicitor and still have had his army career.

Ah, but you forget, she admonished herself, without the wealth that came with the marriage, there would be no property to manage. Neither for him, nor for you. In effect, you were both coerced.

The difference is that I no longer mind having been coerced. But I fear he does. . . .

# Twenty-one

Emily's ball, held in one of London's most respectable hotels, proved to be a spectacular social event.

Spectacular—for everyone but the belle of the ball.

It started out fine.

In a gown of ivory silk trimmed with gold embroidery, a gold ribbon twined through her honey-colored curls, and wearing a simple gold chain and locket, Emily did not fit the pearls-and-pristine-white of most debutantes. A dinner party at Markholme House prior to the ball went well. Emily requested Captain Hendley as her dinner partner, though Charles would lead her out for the first dance at the ball.

Later, she knew the precise moment the evening lost its glow. It was at the end of her second dance, a waltz, with Hendley. The music stopped as Emily and her partner neared an open terrace door.

"Do let us catch a breath of fresh air," Emily said, fanning herself with more vigor than decorum and not waiting for Richard to agree. Several other couples had the same idea, but Emily and Richard found a secluded spot at the end of the balustrade away from the light of open windows.

Emily leaned over the balustrade to look out and up at the sky. "Look, Richard. If you can avoid the lights here, the stars are wonderful!"

He leaned out, too, his body very near hers and as she

pulled back in, their faces nearly touched. They looked into each other's eyes.

"Yes, they are quite wonderful," he said, but she did not think he referred to the stars in the sky. He put a hand gently under her chin to raise her mouth to his.

His lips were soft as he slanted them over hers, but when she responded openly, welcoming him, they became firm and demanding. Yearning and promise, giving and fulfillment marked a brief moment. He pulled away abruptly.

"My apologies, Emily. I should not have done that."

"Why? I wanted you to. And," she challenged, "you enjoyed it as much as I did."

"Yes, I did. But it is not proper, and you know it."

"Sometimes, Captain Hendley, you worry too much about what is proper and improper."

"And sometimes, Miss Longbourne, you do not worry about it enough." He mimicked her tone. "You surely do not want to become the latest *on dit* for the *ton*."

"No." The gossip about Sarah had died down, but would be quickly revived if Lady Markholme's sister were caught in a compromising situation. Hendley stepped away from her and leaned his elbows on the balustrade in front of him.

"However," he said, facing out to the dimly lit garden beyond the terrace, "I am glad to have this moment alone with you, for I have something to tell you."

"What?" She took a shallow breath.

Straightening, he looked at her, then said bluntly, "I have requested a posting to India."

"India! But—but . . . why? You have not mentioned such at all in these last weeks. I—I thought our friendship . . . well, you could have at least . . . Why did you not tell me?" She turned to hide the tears that welled.

"I am telling you now," he said patiently. "My family is still in India. I will join my father's regiment."

"And there is nothing to keep you here, is there?" A trace of angry bitterness crept into her voice.

He put his hand under her elbow, gently turning her

toward him. He reached to toy with a curl at the side of her face. "On the contrary. Were circumstances different, there is much that would keep me here."

She looked into his face, seeing her own despair and longing reflected in his eyes.

"I cannot offer for you, Emily. And I cannot stay here to see you belong to another."

"You do care, then."

"Yes. Very much. But . . . Emily, please. Try to understand." He put his hands to either side of her face, his thumbs wiping away a tear from beneath each eye.

"But not enough." Her tone was flat. "Come, we had better go in." She turned abruptly, then paused to take a breath and brace her shoulders.

She danced every dance remaining on the program and went into supper with no less than a marquis. She laughed. She chatted. She flirted. She received lavish compliments graciously. But afterward, she did not remember what had been said or by whom, what she ate, or even what dances she had performed.

She only remembered Richard's kiss and that he was going away.


Charles had returned to his militia regiment, so Sarah alone perceived their sister's unhappiness. Captain Hendley called twice. On the first occasion, Emily made no attempt to grant him any time alone. On the second, she arranged to be out driving with another. She did not discuss what it was that troubled her, and Sarah hesitated to invade her privacy. Emily would talk when she was ready.

The Markholmes, along with the rest of London able to do so, sought relief from summer heat in country dwellings. Sarah and Matthew welcomed the move; both wanted to oversee their projects in Derbyshire.

Renovation of Markholme Hall was not complete when the family returned. Therefore, they all moved into Rosemont for a few weeks. Rosemont was certainly roomy enough for ordinary family activities, but the library, which had always doubled as an office for Sarah and her grandfather, now seemed inordinately cramped for her and Matthew.

Each actively pursued the project of choice—she, the pottery, and he, the brewery. Matthew liked and trusted Mr. Sinclair, whom he met on returning to Derbyshire. He was, however, determined to bring his own idea of a brewery to fruition. Sarah was equally determined the pottery should be a successful venture. Not fully conscious they were doing so, they entered into a subtle competition. Neither took any pleasure in setbacks for the other, but they did relish their own successes.

Now fully aware of his wife's managerial abilities, Matthew no longer had any of the doubts that had prompted him to suggest she leave such duties to a man. On the surface, the Earl of Markholme and his countess had achieved a close working relationship.

However, they had not recaptured the easy camaraderie of the days before his return to the Peninsular campaign. They took part in family entertainments, but nightly chess games, shared glasses of wine, and idle discussions which had marked the first weeks of their marriage were gone.

The only place they truly bridged the chasm between them was in bed. But even here, there was restraint, each holding back, fearful of giving too much, or having what was offered received with indifference. Matthew visited his wife's bed regularly, but she felt he was making love *to* her rather than *with* her. She was reluctant to initiate romantic overtures.

Knowing she was not his bride of choice, she wondered if he dreamed of a silvery-haired blonde with emerald eyes when he was with his wife. Would he forsake the marital bed once an heir was on the way? Much as she found the present situation wanting, she could not face losing him entirely.

Missing the closeness they once shared, Matthew was at a loss as to how to restore it. His wife never refused him her body, and she participated actively in their encounters. Nevertheless, he felt she was being the dutiful wife rather than the eager lover of before. Despite knowing full well she had been a virgin when they married, and despite his own vows to himself and assurances to her that the past was past, doubt continued to gnaw away at him. Had she not been denied the husband she wanted when Robert died? And was it not possible she had been unfaithful to the husband she was forced to accept?

Nor could he come to terms with why that should matter to him now. No harm had come of whatever had happened. *Their* agreement could proceed as originally outlined.

Still, something was lacking and he wanted at least what they had had in the beginning.

One day as they were both in the library in their now customary separated togetherness—she seated at what had once been her grandfather's desk and he at the massive library table—there was a knock on the door. On instructions to enter, the butler made his announcement.

"My lord, my lady, there are some . . . uh . . . persons who wish to be known to you. The name is MacGowan."

Before Sarah could react, Matthew jumped up from the table and rushed out the door. "MacGowan!" he called. "And Mrs. MacGowan. Come in." He ushered them into the library. "Sarah, you remember the MacGowans—you met them on the dock at Portsmouth—"

"And they saved your life at Toulouse," she interrupted. "Of course I remember them. Welcome." Inviting them to sit down, she rang for refreshments.

Matthew had told Sarah that Maggie was the one who discovered him injured on the battlefield. Afterward, Maggie and Coop had nursed him back to health as Tommy and Hendley foraged for the five of them in the conquered city.

Tommy and Maggie MacGowan now sat close to each other on the settee, apparently to lend each other moral support in these unfamiliar, elegant surroundings.

"What brings you to Derbyshire, MacGowan?" Matthew asked. "I thought surely you would return to that 'wee village in Scotland.' "

"Well, we thought to, that's sure," Tommy replied. "But the truth is there just ain't no work to be had there. We heard there was lotsa work in Manchester, but when we got there, 'twasn't true. Leastways, not anymore. Same thing in Leeds—and Liverpool. Met some o' me mates from the regiment, though, an' one of the fellers said as how you was buildin' a brewery. I happens to have experience in that line an' I got hopes you might could use me." He heaved a sigh after delivering what appeared to be a prepared speech.

"After all that we have been through together, I am certain there is a place for you," Matthew assured him.

"Thank you, my lord."

"But that ain't the only reason we come so far," Maggie said. She seemed embarrassed and cleared her throat. She looked at her husband and went on when he gave her a slight nod. She dug into a battered reticule and handed over to Matthew the ornate gold watch Sarah had given him.

"Well, I'll be . . ." Matthew said. "I thought those ghouls robbing bodies on the battlefield had taken this."

"No, sir. I took it to keep 'em from doin' that and then I just plumb forgot it with ever'thin' else what was goin' on. I'm that sorry, I am. I knowed 'twas important to ye, with her ladyship's picture an' all. Especially after the way you kept callin' for her when you was unconscious." She gave him and Sarah an embarrassed glance.

"Now, Maggie-darlin'," Matthew said, putting her at ease by recalling those weeks in Toulouse when they had all deliberately aped her husband's favorite way of addressing her. "You need not be embarrassed. I am pleased to have the watch back, of course. And I thank you most sincerely."

Lofton brought in the tray then and the MacGowans were persuaded to take tea with Lord and Lady Markholme, "just as nice as you please" as Maggie would regale her neighbors for years afterward. Lofton was instructed to send for Howard who would see that the MacGowans were assigned accommodation and that Tommy would have a job with the brewery.

When the MacGowans had left and the tray was removed, Matthew returned to his seat at the library table. Sarah stood at the window and observed him turn the watch over and over in his hand. She knew they were both thinking of the day she had presented him that gift.

"Nice of them to return the watch," she said, making conversation.

"Yes. They might have sold it and lived off the proceeds for a year or more. From the looks of them, they needed the money right enough. Can you imagine what courage it must have taken for them to return it?"

"I think, given your history with them, they never once thought seriously of not returning it to you."

"Probably." He looked at her thoughtfully. He felt closer to her, knowing she admired the basic goodness of these people as he did. She looked away first, then glanced back at him with a tentative smile.

"They seemed intimidated at first. Then you called her 'Maggie-darlin' and they both relaxed. I liked that."

"They are fine people, Sarah. We came to know each other quite well when Maggie and Coop were tending me—and Tommy and Richard were fending for all of us. I owe them more than I can ever hope to repay."

"As do I," she said softly.

Their eyes locked for a long moment.

"Well . . ." She lifted her hands in a small gesture and started back to the desk.

"Sarah?" He reached out to pull her onto his lap. His husky voice held a trace of his old teasing as he asked, "Does that mean you really are glad to have me back?"

She put her arms around his neck and pressed her forehead to his. "More than you can ever know," she said in a solemn voice.

His arms tightened around her as he brought his lips to hers. It started as a gentle way of saying "welcome back" for both of them, but then fierce desire took over, each expressing urgent need to lay claim to the other.

He moved his hand to caress her breast. She was wearing a low-necked dress with little puff sleeves which he slid with ease down her arms to reveal the rounded swell of her breasts at the neckline. He trailed kisses down her throat and over the exposed part of her breasts.

"Oh, Matthew," she moaned, her hands worked their way through his hair and held him close. She arched her back slightly to press toward the infinite pleasure he was evoking.

"Sarah? I want you."

"Here?" Her tone was disbelieving as she came to her senses, but she could feel his need and her own was equally urgent.

"Yes, here. Now." He rose to stand her on her feet, strode to the door which he quickly locked and came back to her. He knelt on the floor. "Come." He pulled her down beside him on the thick Oriental carpet.

This was not the slow familiar lovemaking they so often engaged in. This was the fierce coupling of two hungry beings, each finding satisfaction in what the other gave, demanding and offering alike.

They lay there for a while, both spent, each savoring the moment. Neither had said a word since he locked the door. Finally, he raised himself and looked into her eyes, half fearing what he might see there.

What he saw was an embarrassed twinkle that sparked a sheepish grin from him. He hugged her to him.

"Please do not say you regret this," he murmured.

"No regrets at all. But you must admit we were a bit carried away. I mean—in the library in the middle of the afternoon! Such behavior is not quite proper, I'm sure." She gave him a smile at once brilliant and seductive.

"Keep looking at me like that and we may get carried away again."

"Tonight, my darling."

"Tonight." He kissed her again.

She sat up and wriggled her bodice into some semblance of order as he readjusted his own clothing. After a quick kiss, he unlocked the door and they settled back to their respective tasks in something near the rapport they had had months before.

For the rest of the day, through the family dinner and the gathering in the drawing room later, their eyes often met, sharing the secret of the afternoon and the promise of the night to come.

# Twenty-two

Their afternoon encounter in the library seemed to clear the air for the Earl of Markholme and his countess, who spent more time together now—even time not directly related to estate or family interests. Servants noted their employers more often than not needed only one bed for the night.

The subtle competition over their respective projects continued unabated, but the undercurrent of antagonism was gone. Both were determined to make their own ventures successful, but neither thought about "losing" the contest anymore. Instead, each quietly took pride in the achievements of the other.

Sarah and Matthew moved back into Markholme Hall, Aunt Bess and Emily choosing to stay in Rosemont for the time being. Later, that residence would be leased to a tenant on a long-term basis. Matthew's office, a large room with leather furniture and military memorabilia, was located in a wing removed from the living quarters. Sarah conducted her business either from a desk in her private sitting room or in the library.

"I am not sure I like this arrangement," Matthew said, finding her in her sitting room a day or two after they had moved back into his house.

"Indeed?" Sarah raised an inquiring eyebrow.

"The Rosemont library had certain attractions definitely

lacking in my office. I grew quite fond of that Oriental carpet." He grinned at the way she colored up at this sally.

"Indeed?" she said again. "I suppose Emily and Aunt Bess would be willing to part with it, if it means so much to you."

"Only if you, dear wife, explain to them why."

"Oh, no." She laughed. "We will make do without it."

Returning to his own office, he found Howard waiting for him. They discussed routine business for a few minutes, then Howard said, "My lord, I think you should know Ainsley has been seen in and around Axton these several days."

"Has he now? I thought to be rid of him."

"He hangs around the pubs. Drinks a lot. And not too careful with his mouth. Swears he will have revenge."

"Probably just idle talk."

"I don't know. He's not likely to face up to you, but he could try something underhanded."

"Like what?"

"I don't know. But I don't trust him at all."

"We will keep an eye out. Put night watchmen on the building projects."

"Good idea."


Efficiency and attention to detail had served the army's Major Cameron well. He now brought these qualities to his peacetime interests. As they came to know him, he gained the respect of the villagers and his own tenants.

"His lordship ain't afraid to git his hands dirty."

"Deals with folks openly."

"Yeah, but he don't take kindly to—what'd he call it?—'insubordination.' "

"Got rid of that Pullen feller quick like."

If he did not enjoy the warm devotion accorded his wife, he nevertheless commanded loyalty. The people began to see hope and prosperity for themselves in the changes that had been initiated. Gradually, the villagers reached consensus—the new earl was worthy of their Miss Longbourne.

Late one morning as he returned from the village, Matthew dropped in at the pottery site. He had visited there before, but not often, for he did not want Sarah to think he was checking on her work. Mr. Sinclair talked with two workers in a shed. Plans for the pottery were spread out on a crude table.

"Carry on," he said, when Sinclair would have stopped his conference to attend his lordship.

Matthew studied the sheets on the table. When the two workers left, Matthew was still engrossed in the plans. He looked up at Sinclair with a frown of confusion.

"These are not the plans I saw in London."

"Mostly they are, my lord, though there are a few changes."

"Why? I assume my wife authorized them?"

"Yes, my lord, she did. Said we should hold back some. We should start smaller, but with an eye to expanding later, maybe here—and here." Sinclair pointed to sections on the sheet in front of him.

"Did she say why she wanted to make these changes?"

"Said the plans were perhaps too grandiose to start with, that we might best see how well it succeeded and then we could expand."

"Did you agree with her?"

"Well, I don't think there is any doubt this venture will be a success. Everything is right—location, materials, workers—even the market."

"But—did you agree with her?"

"Not at first," Sinclair said reluctantly. "But then she said as how some of the capital would have to be used elsewhere, so I said smaller was better than not at all."

"I see."

Matthew was thoughtful as he guided his mount homeward. He knew what had happened. Sarah cut back on her own dream to let him realize his. Moreover, she had done it without playing the martyr or flying into a pet—indeed, without even trying to reason him away from his objective.

He spent some time in his office going over accounts and correspondence before seeking his wife. She was in the garden, snipping roses for a table arrangement.

"Hello, Matthew." She smiled at him. "Are these not simply the most gorgeous flowers you ever saw?"

"Lovely." His gaze encompassed her as well as the blooms she held.

"Did you stop at the vicarage? Edward wished to see you."

"I saw him. I also spent some time at the pottery."

"Oh? Is everything all right?"

"For the most part. I had an interesting discussion with Sinclair."

"Oh?"

He could see she was stalling. "Stop saying 'oh?' like that. You have been found out, my dear."

"I am sure I do not know what you are talking about."

"I think you do. Why did you not discuss changes in the pottery plans with me?" he asked, plunging right in. "Come here." He led her to a bench under a huge maple tree, took the basket from her and set it on the ground.

"Are you upset? It has nothing to do with you," she said, not unkindly.

He put an arm around her shoulders. "Sarah, *everything* about our estates and business ventures has to do with me. We—you and I—are not operating as separate entities here." He lifted her chin to force her to look at him. "I will not countermand any of your decisions, but I do expect to be consulted, my dear. Now, tell me why you cut back on the pottery." He expressed no anger, only curiosity.

"The renovations in town—and here, too—were much more costly than we anticipated. I . . . I did not want you to think I was being selfish in building my pottery at the expense of your brewery."

He looked at her thoughtfully. "*Our* pottery and *our* brewery. Tell me, have you consulted our solicitors lately?"

"No, not since your return. Those gentlemen are not comfortable dealing with a woman. Mr. Howard's figures—"

"Deal only with these farms. You did not consider, then, our investments on the 'Change?"

Her eyes questioned him.

"We are not paupers, Sarah. Not even after paying the enormous debts I brought to our partnership."

"Do you truly believe we can finance both the pottery and the brewery as originally planned? Despite all these renovations? What about housing for workers? And the school? Matthew, I may not have had the very latest figures, but I do have a good idea of where we stand financially."

"I did not say we should not practice some economies. But we need not make all cuts in one area. I *have* seen the latest figures. I think we can do it all, though you are right—we must cut back. Everywhere." He squeezed her shoulder and said in a husky voice, "Next time, talk to me, wife."

Her eyes twinkled. "I will, my lord. I promise."

She kissed him quickly and picked up her basket to return to the task of cutting flowers.

Matthew sat where he was for a long time.

The revelations of this day intrigued him. Not the facts and figures of financial matters. No. The fact of Sarah's willingness to make sacrifices for him. *He* wanted to make a brewery work in Derbyshire, so she would help him achieve his goal—even if it meant not realizing her own as planned.

"Talk to me, wife," he had said. Had he spoken to her about the Ridgeley mess? No. He had leapt to a disastrous conclusion. Her response in the library the other day when she abandoned all restraint proved her need for him. He knew no other man had ever elicited such ardor from her.

He did not know what had happened in the Betsworth library. He might never know. But he knew Sarah was incapable of the betrayal gossip and his own doubt laid on her. Never again would he question her honor and integrity. She was not an Annalisa. Nor had her mother's inconstancy shown up in Sarah, who was steadfast and loyal. Sarah—sweet, honorable, generous Sarah—was his and his alone.

When, precisely, had he fallen in love with her?

Probably when you were arguing most vehemently against it, he admitted ruefully. With all concessions to modesty, he knew she found him attractive. But could she ever come to love him?

Summer fought its annual losing battle against the on-slaught of autumn. Leaves were beginning to turn, though they had yet to reach the brilliance of color to inspire po-ets. Mornings were crisp and clear. The season for hunting parties had arrived.

Occasionally Sarah would catch a faraway look on her husband's face. She wondered if he longed to be else-where. One evening in mid-September, she was in her sit-ting room writing a letter. Matthew sprawled nearby on a chaise longue not really reading the book in his hand.

"What would you say, Sarah, were I to invite some men to join me here for the pheasant season? Game seems plen-tiful this year."

After a moment she answered. "Seems a good idea. I know you miss some of your old friends."

"You have no objections?"

"None. In fact, we could make it a genuine house party and invite ladies, too. I am sure Aunt Bess and Emily—and Catherine, too—would be happy to help entertain the la-dies while you gentlemen are out shooting and telling each other outrageous tales."

He stood and walked over to the window, looking out into the dark. "I hope we will do more than that."

"You have an ulterior purpose in mind?" Her tone was half teasing, half serious.

"Yes." He turned to face her. "I hope to capture the attention of at least some members of what is pleased to regard itself as the ruling class in this country. MacGowan's plight in finding employment is but a small indication of what is happening to thousands. People are being driven off the land. Mere poverty is the least of the ills they contend with. Those in positions to help simply must accept their responsibilities."

She rose and came to him, putting her arms around his waist. "Matthew, you are only one person. You are already doing so much."

"We. We are doing." He hugged her to him, resting his chin on top of her head. "But think, Sarah, how much better if others were doing the same. And if they could see it to be in their own self-interest, I have little doubt they would do so."

"You mean to ask members of the *ton* to soil their aristocratic hands in trade?"

"They can work through intermediaries—they always do."

She pulled her head back to smile into his eyes. "I never thought of you as a reformer, your lordship, sir."

"No! If any of this lot thought they were being persuaded to a reformist point of view, they would be mad as hops and reject it out of hand."

"Then how . . ."

"We just show them what is going on here and then deign to answer their questions."

"Devious. Just plant the ideas."

"Yes. Just plant the seeds. Perhaps we can reap some of the harvest when Parliament meets again in the winter."

"It is a good plan, Matthew, and I am proud of you." Her look and voice were sincere. "But I think you should not make a point of the degree to which I have been involved in these projects."

"Why? I believe in giving credit where it is due."

"I know. But there are those who resent or dismiss any venture a woman initiates. Those who matter, like Adrian, may know. But others . . . ? It is, after all, the projects themselves that are important." Her eyes twinkled as she added, "We can take up women's rights later."

He tightened his arms around her and chuckled softly. "Perhaps you are right, my dear. Just consider the opinion held by your own husband less than a year ago. And I am confident you will not allow me to forget that 'later' either!" He kissed her lightly.

"Never."

Two days later, invitations went out for a house party in October. There would be nearly a dozen men in the party who, if not themselves among the most powerful of the nation, had the ears of those who were. Wives and adult children swelled the group to nearly thirty people.

The harvest of field and tree was well under way. Supervising preparations for the house party added to Sarah's duties, and she often questioned where her time had gone in a given day. She began to seek the quiet sanctuary of her chamber of an afternoon, and on at least one occasion Betsy found her asleep at her desk.

"Poor dear. She's trying to do too much, she is," Mrs. Nelson, the housekeeper, opined.

One afternoon, having taken the gig to visit tenants, Sarah and Emily passed through the village and stopped to purchase some ribbons and writing paper. As they were leaving the shop, they encountered Lady Meridon.

"Lady Markholme, I have had the most wonderful news and I simply must share it with you," Lady Meridon fluttered in a voice that had gained nothing in the way of pleasant tones over the summer.

Sarah waited expectantly.

"My family is coming to help me celebrate my birthday. So it appears we shall each have guests in October," Lady Meridon babbled on. "I shall, of course, have a small reception at which you and your guests will be ever so welcome. I shall send you a note."

Sarah murmured her thanks and asked after Lady Meridon's daughter. Back in the gig, she and Emily looked at each other and started to giggle.

"She is a gabble-grinder, is she not?" Emily asked.

"Yes, and you see what she has done? Now I shall have to invite her and her guests to some function of ours. And—oh, Emily—I really do not want to entertain that Poindexter woman." Sarah did not know whether to laugh at how Lady Meridon had outmaneuvered her or wail at the predicament the maneuvering had created. She picked up the reins and the vehicle moved forward.

"I know, Sissy Sarah," Emily said sympathetically, reverting to a childhood endearment. She patted Sarah's shoulder. "After her role in that awful scene at the Betsworth ball, one can understand. But if you give her the cut direct, it will only start the talk again. Never mind, we shall think of something—perhaps a simple 'at home' will suffice. Aunt Bess or Catherine can help put that woman in her place."

In the event, though, it was neither of those two amiable ladies who "put that woman in her place."

# Twenty-three

Having honestly thought a change of scenery would lift Emily's spirits, Sarah was saddened by her sister's continued unhappiness. Besides increased household duties, Emily willingly took on a greater role in seeing to the needs of tenants and helping in the parish school. Sarah surmised that Emily threw herself into these activities to take her mind off more distressing concerns.

The two were strolling one afternoon in the gardens at Rosemont.

"You know, Em, it might help if you talked about it."

"About what?"

"Whatever it is that bothers you. That has troubled you for weeks now. Perhaps I or someone else can help."

"No one can help. It is not a fixable problem. All my life I have been able to run to someone—you, Grandpapa, Aunt Bess—to have my hurts mended, but not this time."

Sarah persisted. "I suspect this has something, everything, to do with Captain Hendley."

"Yes, it does. But there is nothing to be done. I imagine I will get over it in a decade or two." She smiled at her own joke, but the smile did not reach her eyes.

"You love him, then?"

"Yes. Would that I did not, but as you once told me, we cannot dictate to our hearts. Do I disappoint you?"

"Disappoint me? No. I am disappointed *for* you, perhaps. I had hoped for a grander match for you. But Richard is a fine person."

"With whom there will be no match at all."

"You are certain of that?"

"Yes. His exact words were 'I cannot offer for you, Emily.' He applied for a posting to India."

"India!"

"India," Emily repeated dully.

"He accepted our invitation for the house party, though."

"I suppose he is coming to tender his farewell. He is very fond of Matthew, you know."

"Shall you be very uncomfortable?" Sarah wished to spare Emily further distress.

"No. I am learning to accept those things in life that cannot be changed. But, oh, Sarah, it hurts so much!" There were tears in her voice. Sarah put her arms around her to offer comfort, however futile.

That night Sarah brought up the topic of Emily's happiness—or lack of it—to Matthew. They were lying in Matthew's huge bed casually talking and Matthew was nearly asleep.

"Did you know Captain Hendley requested a posting to India?" she asked.

"Yes. He discussed it with me."

"Did you encourage him to do so?"

"Not exactly. But I did not discourage him, either. He will join his father's regiment there." Matthew yawned.

"Is he leaving England because of Emily?"

"He didn't say. I suspect she is a factor, though."

"Is he in love with her?"

"He did not say so." Reluctantly giving up on sleep at the moment, he turned toward her and slipped his arm beneath her head, drawing her closer. "Why do you ask?"

"Because she loves him and is quite brokenhearted."

"At her age people do get over broken hearts."

"But why should she if he is in love with her, too? I cannot think this is just a passing infatuation."

"Sarah, you were the one who insisted she must make a better match than Hendley could offer." Matthew's tone carried the impatience invariably manifested by males confused by their mates.

"I did not realize she loved him."

"What has love to do with it? You wanted her to have a title and the comfort wealth could bring her."

"How could she be happy if she were in love with someone else—no matter how rich she might be?"

"Other people have been."

This gave her pause. Was Matthew telling her he was happy in his own marriage? Or, that he was resigned to it though he was in love with someone else? Had he not just suggested love was irrelevant?

"I doubt Emily could be happy in such a marriage. And I do want her to be happy."

"What would you have me do, Sarah? I cannot order him to marry her. I could not even have done so when I was still his commanding officer."

"I know. I did not intend that it become a problem for you to solve."

"Hmmm. I may have a solution," he said slowly, still thinking. "You are absolutely certain of her feelings?"

"Yes. Why? What are you thinking?"

"We still need a replacement for Ainsley." He waited for her to react.

"Steward? Could Richard do that job? Would he?"

"No doubt he could. Would? I don't know. He once said he would never leave the army. There is a long army tradition in his family—three or four generations."

She was quiet for a moment. "It is rather daunting to interfere in others' lives. Do we have the right, Matthew?"

"Make up your mind, woman." He laughed softly. "In any event, all we can do is make the offer. He and Emily must work out their own difficulties." He pulled her closer and began to trail small kisses across her face and down her neck. "As victims of more autocratic meddling our-selves, we did not do so badly, did we?" He punctuated this question with his mouth seeking hers.

"I thought you were going to sleep," she said after a while.

"I was. But you have awakened a sleeping giant and you must pay the price."

"A giant, is it?" She giggled and caressed the most awak-ened part of him. "Gracious, I do believe it is. Well, never let it be said the countess of Markholme does not pay her debts."

When Sarah awoke the next morning, Matthew had al-ready gone. She sat up, swung her legs from beneath the covers, and promptly fell back in a near swoon. She willed herself to lie still as a wave of nausea passed through her innards. She pulled the bell rope to summon Betsy.

"Are you all right, my lady? You look so pale."

"I will be fine. Just bring me some tea and toast, please. And, Betsy,"—she waited for the maid to turn to face her, then added sternly—"not a word of this to anyone. You hear? Not a word."

"Oh, yes, mum."

Sarah lay back to await the restorative tea.

A babe. She had suspected for some time, but now she was certain. She grinned foolishly. I know just when it hap-pened, too. Matthew is going to love that library carpet even more now.

She sobered. Last night he had spoken of being a victim of others' meddling. Did he find the marriage burden-some, then? He will have his heir. Will this child spell the end of any happiness with my husband? Oh, please, let it be a girl.

Thereafter, her days fell into a new routine. If she lay very still after waking, and did not try to stir until Betsy had brought tea and dry toast, she could greet the morn-ing without a side trip to the night jar. If Matthew thought it strange that his wife had become such a slugabed, he did not say anything.

Sarah could not bring herself to tell Matthew the news, yet. She was sorely afraid that once he knew a babe was on the way, he would no longer feel it necessary to share so much of her life. How could she face such a possibility?

Adrian appeared two days before the scheduled arrival of other guests. He came directly from a diplomatic mission to Paris and passed along interesting tidbits of news. Sarah excused herself early that night to allow Matthew some special time with his friend. She had scarcely left the drawing room when Adrian said, "I saw Ridgeley in Paris."

"You did?" Ridgeley was not a topic Matthew welcomed. "I thought you went there to see Ambassador Wellington."

"I did. But Ridgeley attended some of the social functions. Insisted that I meet him privately one evening."

"And?"

"I met him. He was drinking heavily, but knew what he was about all the same."

Matthew held up his hand as if to ward off the next words. "I hope you are not about to bring up that tired topic of Ridgeley and Sarah at Betsworths'. Sarah and I have put that behind us."

"Glad to hear it. However, you should listen to this, I think."

"All right." Matthew agreed reluctantly.

"What troubled me most about that whole affair was *why* Ridgeley behaved so dishonorably. I knew it was a setup at the start, but I never understood why he acted so out of character."

"Women drive men to doing strange things," Matthew said with a shrug.

"Yes. And that is what happened, though not in the way you mean."

"Oh?"

"He was up to his ears in debt. Creditors threatened to

send him to debtors' prison. And there were gaming debts as well."

"Not so unusual."

"His cousin paid them all after that scene in the Betsworth library."

"Annalisa." Matthew's voice was flat.

Adrian nodded. "She apparently had—or has—this fixation about you. Thought if Sarah were compromised, you'd seek comfort in familiar arms."

"So why was the noble Ridgeley unburdening himself to you at this point?"

"Who knows? Conscience, maybe. Said he'd heard the plan came to naught. Anyway, he's pretty miserable. Pathetic, really."

"Too bad," Matthew said without a trace of sympathy.


Quite suddenly, it seemed to Sarah, the house filled with people requiring attention. These days, too, fell into a routine. Entertaining so many turned out to be surprisingly less demanding than she had anticipated—thanks to her female relatives. The big event of each day was dinner at which Sarah changed the seating daily. Card games, charades, and music dominated the evenings.

Within days, the visitors were at ease with each other. Even Lady Rexton, the most difficult guest, told Sarah she had "rarely felt so comfortable in someone else's home."

One day, rather than join the others in the hunt, Adrian appropriated Matthew's office, writing letters and memos to be sent with a footman to catch the post. After lunch he sought Sarah's company for a stroll in the garden.

"You seem in especially good looks these days, Sarah."

"Thank you. The country air agrees with all of us."

"I would venture to guess there is more than country air involved."

Was her secret out? How could he know? "W-w-what do you mean?"

"You and Matthew seem to be more in charity with each other than you were in the city."

She breathed an inward sigh of relief. "Removing to the country—away from the scene of the crime, so to speak—helped. We have, as you can see, been very busy."

"And you are doing some very good work, too. Rexton has been won over and Lindford is interested."

"Matthew tells me they ask the right questions."

"But he will need the third member of the triumvirate to carry his ideas in Parliament."

"Who is . . . ?"

"Poindexter." He paused, then went on, "I know that is not a name you wish to hear. But the truth is, Poindexter is a very powerful contender in the political arena."

"My grandfather respected him," she admitted, "but I always thought it was for his savvy about horses."

"Poindexter likes to gainsay the opposition by pretending to be little more than a dilettante sportsman, but he is actually a very astute fellow—and he is remarkably close to the Prime Minister."

"Oh, dear." Her sigh was audible this time. "Matthew needs the husband and the wife hates me. What an interesting dilemma."

"For what it may be worth, I do not think that wife has much influence in her husband's political affairs. She has little knowledge, and less interest, in such matters. And I think she can be neutralized."

"You do?"

"Yes," he said firmly, but he did not elaborate.


Sarah had another little *tête-à-tête* with a gentleman. At her invitation, Charles joined her in her sitting room one morning after the others had left for the day's sport—and after Sarah had recovered from her daily bout of nausea.

He threw up his hands in mock defense as he entered the room. "I'm innocent. I swear I did not do it."

"Oh, do sit down and try to behave." Hers was an equally mocking show of exasperation.

"All right. Just please don't beat me."

"I want to ask you a question," she said, her tone now serious, "and I want absolute truth."

He was instantly serious himself. "As you wish."

"Are you happy with this military career of yours? Six months, more or less, is not a long time, but you must have some idea of whether you like it."

"Yes, Sarah, I am very happy with it. There are times when they set us to doing things as boring as can be—but my guess is that would be true in anything. Rest easy, Sarah. You have helped me to exactly the life I want."

"Good."

"And just what would you have done if I had said I was miserable?" he teased.

"Why, of course, I should have done all I could to get you out of it." She was still very serious.

"I truly believe you would. Is this the same big sister who once told Emily and me we must accept the consequences of our actions?" He affected the tone she must have used at the time.

"Well, that was different. You were being punished for letting the Petersons' pig invade their vegetable patch."

"The principle is the same," he said with more maturity than she had ever observed in him before. "I could not give up at this point if I were dissatisfied. And I am not."

"I am very glad to hear it." Well, she thought, at least this part of her bargain with Matthew had worked out.

"And now you." He held her gaze with his own. "Are you satisfied with the life Grandfather's will forced on you? I still think he was terribly unfair to you."

"Yes. Very satisfied. And I am very happy!" The statement was out before she thought to guard her tongue.

Charles paused. Then a light of recognition dawned in his eyes. "You're in love with him! Aren't you? That's wonderful!"

"It would be wonderful—if he felt the same way. But he does not."

"How do you know? Have you told him? Have you asked him?"

"No, of course not. I have more pride than that! And you are not to say anything to him, either. Promise me. Promise me, Charles!"

"All right, I promise. But, Sarah, don't allow your pride to ruin your happiness." He rose, squeezed her shoulder warmly, and left the room.

# Twenty-four

It was several days before Matthew found opportunity to speak privately with Richard Hendley.

"Are you still determined to join the forces in India?" Matthew asked as Hendley joined him in the library.

"Yes. I believe it will advance my career."

"Am I to understand your feelings in a certain quarter have altered, then?" Matthew knew Hendley might rightfully take offense at such prying.

Hendley looked at him directly. Matthew read pain and regret before the younger man looked away. "No. They have not. But one accepts what he cannot change."

"Do you think you would find civilian life miserably boring if you were to give up the army?"

"No. Probably not. But I've lived with the army one way or another all my life. I like it. It is in my blood."

"It does have its rewards, I will grant. But so does life on this other side."

"In your case, you mean. But there is simply nothing for me as a civilian. You, of all people, are aware of how hard it is for returning soldiers. Look at poor MacGowan. Officers have it no easier."

"You may remember my telling you some weeks ago that the knowledge and skills you showed in the Peninsula could be useful in civilian life."

"Yes. I admit the idea intrigued me. But I see no pressing need for my services among the body politic."

"Perhaps not. But *I* have such a need."

"You? Surely not. You appear to have sufficient help. I will not have you making a place for me. I am not a charity case, my lord."

"That is not at all what I had in mind." Having noted the stiffening in both tone and posture of the young man, Matthew kept his voice carefully impersonal. "You know I dismissed the Markholme steward."

"Howard is an able man, though."

"He is—for the agricultural side of things. But he is getting on in years. I shall certainly rely upon him for what he can do for as long as he can do it, but I need to look to the future. The pottery, the brewery, the farms, interests in London—not to mention other holdings of this earldom—require constant attention. Sarah and I have a genuine need for someone to share in this task."

"And you just happened to think of poor, poverty-laden Hendley?" Now his tone was resentful.

"Look." Matthew's tone turned edgy. "I will, in fact, come by the help I need. You and I worked so well together for king and country doing much the same thing, I thought of you. But, if you are not interested . . . so be it."

"I cannot say I am not interested." Hendley spoke slowly, his voice rather flat. "But I am curious to know what Miss Longbourne has to do with your offer."

"The girl seems quite taken with you. Concern for her happiness was a factor in making this offer to you."

Hendley's face flushed with anger. "I cannot credit that the lovely Emily is having you buy her a husband!"

"Emily knows nothing of this proposal. Should you take the position, you are on your own with her."

"Thank you, my lord," Hendley said stiffly. "But I cannot take this position. I will not be a charity case and I will not be bought as a trinket for some society girl."

" 'Some society girl'? I had thought you cared for her more deeply that. Sorry. I misunderstood." Matthew rose to end the interview. The young man before him was the picture of wounded pride, and Matthew wondered how he might have handled the offer differently. "I shall have to fill this position by the first of the year. If you change your mind . . ."

"I will not be changing my mind," Hendley said emphatically. Then, rising to extend his hand, he added in a voice that was politely false, "But I do thank you for the offer. Now, if you will excuse me . . ."

Before Hendley was out the door, though, Matthew had the last word. "You know, Richard, sometimes pride gets in the way of some quite wonderful things in life."

Therein lies a lesson for you, too, Cameron, he mused.

Sarah longed to make excuses not to attend Lady Meridon's reception. As it was, too many of her own guests, not to mention other gentry in the district, would have viewed her absence as highly irregular. And, Matthew wanted to be there. She could not dispel the nagging thought that Matthew's eagerness might be prompted by the very thing that made her reluctant to go—the presence of Poindexter's wife.

Sarah and Matthew had never discussed Annalisa. Did he harbor regrets for what might have been? Did he long for the beautiful Annalisa instead of the wife willed to him?

Betsy was trying to control her ladyship's rebellious curls when Matthew came to the dressing room door, ready to go down.

"I could still wish for some way to avoid this particular obligation," Sarah said.

"Short of a death in the family or a surprise visit from the Prince Regent, I do not see how it may be done." He smiled.

"I know." If she had been the sort to pout, Sarah would have felt perfectly free to do so now.

"Are you not well, Sarah? You seem so out of sorts lately. Maybe this house party was too much after all."

She caught Betsy's eye in the looking glass and gave the

maid a barely perceptible shake of her head. She was immediately contrite. "No. I am fine, my lord. Truly I am. I am sure we will all have an enjoyable time."

"Let us hope so."

Lady Meridon's "reception" was a good deal grander than its name implied. The hostess was gracious, simpering, and fawning—her demeanor dictated entirely by the rank and gender of whichever guest she was greeting. Much of the furniture had been removed from a large formal drawing room which was decorated with fall foliage and she had hired three musicians to provide music for dancing. In an adjoining room, card games flourished for those so inclined. Later, there would be a light supper.

Sarah watched as Matthew casually sought the ear of Lord Poindexter to invite him and Dalrymple to join the shooting party the next day. The hunters would just happen to ride by the brewery and the pottery on their way to the field. The ladies were all invited to join the gentlemen for tea later in the afternoon. Sarah had girded herself for this encounter with the woman who had tacitly declared herself the countess of Markholme's Nemesis.

She was engaged in a comfortable coze with Aunt Bess and two other ladies when the musicians changed their program from subdued background music to more lively strains for dancing. Sarah was pleased and flattered when her husband, having given Poindexter over to another guest, immediately sought her for the dance.

"Well?" she said, as they swung into a waltz.

"Well, what?" He smiled down at her.

"Did you persuade the great man that reform is necessary?"

"Not yet. But he is thinking about it."

"All worthwhile endeavors must start somewhere," she said primly. They danced in silence for a few moments, then Matthew spoke, his voice sincere.

"Thank you."

"For what?"

"For supporting me in this. It means so much to those fellows returning from the wars."

She was flustered by his praise. "I am glad you are able to help so many of them."

"But it could not happen without you," he said. Warmth and pleasure swirled through her. She looked up at him with no attempt to hide her emotions. She squeezed the hand holding hers and moved the other higher on his shoulder to toy with the hair just touching his collar. He pulled her closer, not missing a step. Nor did she.

"Matthew!" she said in her best lady-of-the-manor tone.

"What?" He grinned.

"This is not proper behavior, and you know it."

"You started it." He pulled her even closer.

"I most certainly did not," she protested, moving her hand from the nape of his neck to just above his elbow, and pulling back a little.

"Did too," he argued, not allowing her the distance she strove for, but still not missing a beat. He grinned wickedly and bent down to whisper directly into her ear. "But we can finish it later, my love."

When she colored up, he laughed aloud and swung her into the final swirls of the dance.

Matthew returned his wife to her friends and was striding across the room toward a group that included Trenville and Hendley, when he was accosted by Lady Poindexter. He gave a polite, insincere smile and would have moved on, but she stopped him.

"La, Matthew. Surely you are not going to ignore an old friend, are you?"

Matthew recognized her flirtatious tone in a voice that carried more than was strictly decorous in this surrounding. She had drawn the attention of several people. Among them was her husband who had been standing some distance from her when she detained Lord Markholme. Over

Annalisa's shoulder, Matthew saw Poindexter move close enough to overhear his wife's conversation.

"Your ladyship," Matthew said, carefully avoiding standing too close to her.

"It is imperative that I speak with you. Meet me in the library in five minutes," she said urgently, her voice considerably lower now.

"May I know the nature of this imperative?"

"Please, Matthew, just meet me."

The desperate plea in her voice was reflected in her eyes. This was a different Annalisa, not at all the self-assured sophisticate. He was reminded poignantly of the young Annalisa of a previous life. He wanted to ignore her, to tell her to leave him alone, but perhaps he owed her a hearing. And perhaps he could put an end to her causing pain to Sarah. He reluctantly agreed to meet her.

He instinctively looked to where Sarah was sitting. She did not seem to notice him conversing with Annalisa.

Five minutes later, as he entered the Meridon library, Lady Poindexter stood alone by the fireplace. A candelabrum sat on a table nearby shedding limited light. Oh, lord. He should not have agreed to this. If he and Annalisa were discovered here and now, how would it look to others?

She moved seductively toward him, her eyes fixed on him unnaturally.

"I understand we are to have tea together, Matthew." She made it sound as though the two of them would have some sort of tryst.

"The entire Meridon party has been invited to join our twenty-odd guests at Markholme," he said evenly. He deliberately kept distance between them.

"With such a crowd of people, we will have little time to ourselves, then. You must know I came to Derbyshire expressly to be with you again."

"I had rather thought you to be accompanying your husband on a visit to a relative."

"Of course. But is it not wonderful that you and I can

thus meet without incurring such unpleasant gossip as followed your wife and *her* lover? They were most indiscreet to allow themselves to be caught. But we need fear no detection. I made sure no one knows about us." She again moved toward him, extending her hand to touch him. Again, he sidestepped to avoid the physical contact.

"Lady Poindexter," he said firmly, "I fear you are laboring under some misapprehension about the character of my wife and, indeed, about my feeling for both her and you."

She laughed and the sound was brittle. "I think not, my lord. I was, after all, your first love. I know you perhaps better than you know yourself."

Matthew heaved an exasperated sigh. How did one deal with such obvious refusal to see reality? "Once, when we were both much younger and I was very foolish, I thought myself in love with you. Indeed, I was so very stupid as to think you might return my affection in kind. Thank God, you did not." His tone here was remarkably fervent.

"You welcome rejection? Why?" Beneath her instant anger, curiosity shone as well.

"I should then have missed knowing my Sarah."

"Come now, Matthew. The whole *ton* knows your marriage was a forced affair. You cannot pass it off as a love match at this late date." Again, her brittle laugh invaded the room. "Nor can you ignore the fact that 'your' Sarah actively cuckolded you while you were away."

"I care nothing—nothing—for what the *ton* may say of my marriage. I have made clear to you on more than one occasion this matter is strictly between Sarah and me."

"And her affair with my cousin Ridgeley? Is that between the three of you, then?" Her tone was decidedly nasty now.

"I am glad you brought that up, my lady. I have only recently confirmed my suspicions regarding that incident—and your scheme to discredit my wife."

She blanched. "I—I have no idea what you are talking about."

"Yes, you do." He proceeded to outline Ridgeley's revelations to Trenville.

"It is all lies," she said vehemently. "You cannot prove I had anything at all to do with that scene."

"I doubt it will become necessary to prove it officially. The point is that I believe it to be the truth. I suppose if 'proof' were required, the Betsworth servants who delivered messages to my wife and her sister could be produced. However, the gossip has died down. Under the circumstances, your ladyship, it would be in your best interest to do all you can to ensure it stays dead."

She started to open her mouth for a rejoinder, but closed it.

"I think he has you there, my lady," her husband said, stepping out of the shadows in one corner.

"Victor! My dear, this is not what it seems at all." She unconsciously echoed the very words Sarah had uttered on another occasion. Such irony was lost on the self-absorbed Annalisa.

"Cut line, my dear. I heard it all. I should have reined you in some time ago, but I kept hoping that business with Viscount Bryson had taught you some restraint." He turned to Matthew. "I did not know of my wife's machinations in the aspersions against Lady Markholme, my lord, but I think you may count on Lady Poindexter's cooperation. Nor will you be subjected to further indiscreet importuning such as you have apparently endured in recent months." He paused to look directly at his wife. "She does, after all, presently enjoy a most generous allowance. . . ."

Matthew hardly knew what to say. He gave Poindexter a slight bow.

"Come," Poindexter said, taking his wife's arm. "We shall all three rejoin the party. I cannot think anyone will remark upon the three of us having been absent together."

Only a few of the guests even noticed when they returned to the drawing room. As they entered, Poindexter put his hand on Matthew's shoulder in a friendly gesture and said, "By the bye, my lord, I am looking forward to our outing tomorrow. But I fear my wife will be indisposed. She suffers these headaches, you see."

He ignored his wife's barely controlled fury.


Sarah, had, indeed, noticed her husband leave the drawing room and Lady Poindexter's departure immediately afterward. Suspicion confirmed, she noted sadly. Then she was angry. The nerve of the man, playing with her emotions as he had—flirting with her, promising later delights, then leaving the company for a tryst with his erstwhile lover. Why, she had even thought to tell him of the babe tonight.

She also noticed his return with the lady and the lady's husband. Confused, but unwilling to face him or her emotions, she deliberately strolled across the room to speak with her sister when she saw Matthew move toward her. For the rest of the evening, though she danced two sets with others, she avoided any but the most superficial contact with her husband. In the carriage which they shared with two of their house guests, she spoke little and sat as far away from him as possible.

When she would have gone directly to her chamber on their return home, he did not allow it, pulling her into his own and closing the door.

"Now, would you like to tell me why I have been getting a cold shoulder from you the last few hours?"

"I do not know what you are talking about and I do not want to discuss it."

"That makes sense."

"I don't care whether it makes sense. I am tired." She started for the door between their chambers.

"Oh, no." He caught her about the waist and pulled her back against him. "We are going to have this out here and now. You know I met with Annalisa? That *is* what this is about, is it not?"

"Yes, it is." Her tone was icy. "You are not exactly a man of your word, are you, my love?"

"Just what does that mean?" Rigid with anger, he swung her around to face him.

"You once pledged never to knowingly or willingly subject your wife to public ridicule."

"So far as I know, I have not done so now."

"No? Just what do you suppose the whole of England was thinking as they saw you march off with the beautiful Annalisa tonight?"

"The whole of England, was it? What *can* they think when the lady's husband was with us?"

"Was he now?"

"Actually, yes. Though I admit neither Annalisa nor I knew at first that he was there. However, you may rest assured, madam, I did nothing with the lady then—nor, indeed, in the last ten years—to which he, or you, could have objected." He released his hold on her. "But I do most sincerely appreciate the loving trust you have placed in me."

"I assume you mean the same loving trust you placed in me?"

"Touché, madam." He gave a little shrug of defeat and bowed as she flounced out of the room.

Once again, neither the Earl of Markholme nor his countess had much sleep. She could hear him pacing from time to time and once or twice he thought he heard a muffled sob, but he could not be sure.

# Twenty-five

Hendley's presence at Markholme Hall had thrown Emily onto an emotional seesaw. She knew her own heart well enough and she was sure he returned her feelings. He had made it very clear, though, that he would not offer for her when his prospects were so dim. Nor would he allow her to accept a lower standard of living.

Her usual ebullient self, Emily greeted him with pleasure and cheer along with the other guests. She was determined that no one, least of all Richard Hendley, should see the degree of her unhappiness. She chatted with him, danced with him, rode with him, but there were no private meetings, no kisses.

The day after the Meridon reception, Emily knew the men had planned an early morning hunt. She was surprised when Lofton appeared in the breakfast room to announce that Captain Hendley wished to see Miss Longbourne.

"I shall come with you," Aunt Bess said, laying her serviette aside.

"No, finish your breakfast, Aunt," Emily said. "I will see what it is he wants. Probably just a message from the Hall. We need not stand on ceremony with Captain Hendley."

"If you are sure, my dear . . ." Aunt Bess could not suppress the doubt of one schooled in the proprieties of a previous generation.

Emily found him in the library seated near the fireplace. He rose as she entered.

"Hello, Richard. You have a message from the Hall?"

"No. I came on my own account." His eyes seemed to devour her and she wished she had donned something besides a rather aged pink muslin gown that morning.

"On your own account?"

"Yes. I wanted to say goodbye to you privately and I fear there will be little chance of doing so later in the day. I intend to return to London tomorrow."

"Tomorrow? I thought the house guests were staying another week yet."

"Others are. But something has come up. I must leave sooner." He did not look at her.

"I see," she said doubtfully, not seeing at all. "Your posting to India?"

"Well, yes. There is much to be done before I embark."

"Richard? Is something wrong? Are you not happy about returning to India?"

"No. I mean, yes." He smiled ruefully. "No, nothing is wrong. Yes, I am glad about the posting." But Emily did not believe him. He seemed agitated and nervous.

"I shall miss you," she said sadly, feeling tears threaten.

"Ah, Emily," he groaned, "if only things were different for us." He gathered her in his arms and pressed his face against her neck. "I shall never forget you. Never."

She hugged him tightly, then pulled back so she could look into his eyes. She spoke slowly and deliberately, holding his gaze all the while. "Richard, what if I were to come to India? Aunt Bess has a cousin in Rajastan."

She saw hope leap into his eyes before he controlled his expression. "Come to India? You can't do that! You belong here. Life is not easy there. Single women come to India to find husbands when they have failed to do so here at home. You will have no trouble finding one here."

"If I wanted one here, I could already be planning a wedding. I *will* go to India. If you want to ignore me once

I am there, so be it. But I love you, Richard, and I think you love me . . ."

"Yes, I do," he said with more pain than joy.

"Then why on earth must we be apart?"

"You know why."

"No, I don't. It's your pride, isn't it? Your silly pride that values shallow wealth and social position over our feelings for each other." The tears welled over.

"Ah, Emily, please don't cry." His own voice was full of anguish. "I cannot take you away from your family and home to a life of blistering hot sun, interminable dust, inadequate housing. The Indian people are either very rich or desperately poor. We would be desperately poor, too, by English standards."

She twisted out of his arms and stood before him. "We could make it. With your salary and my marriage portion, we could do it. But, no. The ever-so-virtuous Captain Hendley could not accept that. If you are miserable without me—and I do hope you are—you keep remembering that it was your choice, not mine."

With that, she started to leave the room, but, reaching the door, she turned back. She reached up, pulled his head down to hers, and kissed him soundly on the lips. "Goodbye, Richard. Safe journey," she whispered and, before he could react, she was gone.

Richard Hendley heaved a heart-wrenching sigh and sank into the chair he had occupied earlier. Never in his life had he had cause to doubt himself as he did at this moment. First Matthew, now Emily accused him of letting pride keep him from what he really wanted.

And what was it, exactly, that he really wanted? Emily? Most assuredly. And the army career? Face it, Hendley, he told himself. You went into the army because you grew up with it, because your parents expected it of you. It was never the army as a way of life, the army as a tradition that you found rewarding—it was the work you did in it, the challenge of solving day-to-day problems. Perhaps Matthew was right, civilian life held its share of such challenges, too. Wasn't his pursuit of the army career at this point just an excuse, a defense motivated by pride?

Needing time to think, he left Rosemont to spend the rest of the day riding aimlessly and pondering. He thought of Emily's threat to follow him to India. He was humbled by the idea that she would willingly give up so much merely to be with him. And he? What would he give up to achieve the same end? In this case, giving might mean accepting, too. Accepting Emily's love and giving her his all in return. Accepting Matthew's offer and then giving the best performance he could.

After dinner, he asked to speak with Matthew privately.

Hendley entered the Markholme library feeling like a schoolboy visiting the headmaster's office. His hands were sweaty and he could not seem to still them. Matthew offered him a brandy and when they both had their glasses in hand and were seated, Matthew said, "Well . . . ?"

"I want to apologize for reacting the way I did to your offer the other day."

"Ten years ago, I might have reacted the same way," Matthew said magnanimously. "But just so you know—it was not an offer of charity. I fully expected to receive good return on my investment in you."

"I know that now. I probably knew it when you made the offer, but I just wasn't thinking. And you were right— we did work well together in the Peninsula."

"Does this mean you've changed your mind and will take the job?"

"If the offer is still open, yes. And if I have your permission to ask Emily to marry me—if she'll have me after today."

"I'm glad you changed your mind. As for Emily, that foolish girl is incomprehensibly fond of you." Matthew's eyes twinkled and his affection for Emily showed plainly. "Were I to refuse you permission, Sarah would have my head and Lord knows what Emily might do."

"Follow me to India—at least that is her threat."

"And you quarreled about it? I thought Emily seemed a bit out of sorts this afternoon."

The next morning found Captain Hendley, not on his way to London, but back in the Rosemont library.

"I thought you were leaving today." Emily was surprised to see him. Her voice was carefully controlled.

"I've changed my mind. About a lot of things. Matthew offered me a position as steward, and I am inclined to accept it, though at first I said no."

"What about your plans to return to India and join your father's regiment? I thought the army outweighed everything else in your life."

"Not everything," he said softly, taking her hands in his.

"But will you like being a steward?" she persisted. "I would not have you unhappy in such an important matter."

"Yes," he said sincerely. "I will like it. And I think I will do it well."

"Your modesty is overwhelming." She smiled for the first time since entering the room.

"Emily! Surely you realize what this means?"

"You will stay in England?" Hope was tentative.

"Yes! And we can be married!" He pulled her into his arms. "Please say you will have me." His voice was less confident now.

She locked her hands indecently behind his neck and looked at him directly. Her eyes twinkled.

"What makes you think I would welcome addresses from a lowly steward when I might have a captain in His Majesty's Forces?" She snuggled closer.

"How about an ex-captain?" he asked softly.

"I will . . . consider . . . the offer." She dragged the words out slowly, then immediately and rapidly added, "I have considered."

"And?" His arms tightened around her.

"Yes! I will have you."

Neither could have said afterward whether it was his bending to her lips or her hands pulling his head to hers that resulted in the sealing kiss. Then she said, her voice soft, but firm, "I was serious about going to India, you know."

"I know. Stubborn little thing, aren't you?"

"I love you, Richard."

"And I love you, Emily. More than you can imagine." He kissed her again, his lips gentle, but urging.

Sarah readily shared her sister's joy. She really did want Emily to be happy above any other consideration. However, she could not help thinking that one of the reasons for her own marriage, an advantageous match for Emily, had come to naught. Emily and Richard's delight in each other—manifested in intimate glances, whispered laughter, surreptitious touches—was a poignant reminder to Sarah that she and Matthew had not yet mended the breach between them, though she thought they both wanted to do so.

One afternoon, she sought her husband in his office.

"I wonder if I might talk with you about your new steward and my sister?" she asked tentatively.

"Our." His tone was neutral as he gestured to a seat on the leather-covered couch and seated himself beside her. "*Our* steward and *our* sister."

"Yes. Well . . . *our.* I have been thinking about them a great deal and about the sum we had agreed upon as an eventual marriage settlement for Emily."

"You want to change it?"

"The provisions, not the end result."

"What have you in mind, my dear?"

The endearment pleased her, but she must not allow herself to be distracted. "If we were to grant them residence in Rosemont and the income from the home farm there for their lifetime, would that arrangement not be quite close to her settlement and provide his salary?"

He turned this over in his mind for some time. "You are absolutely right, Sarah. Why did I not see that?"

"This will provide them residence without trying to find other suitable lodging close enough for him to perform his duties as our agent." She smiled as she emphasized the word *our*.

"Income from the home farm. Perfect." He put his arm around her shoulder and hugged her to him. His enthusiasm was contagious and she raised her face for what was to be a quick kiss to acknowledge the agreement. Matthew raised his head and glanced at the clock on the wall.

"Damn. Howard is due here momentarily."

"Regrettable . . . but there is always tonight," she murmured, seeing her own desire reflected in his eyes.

In the next several days many changes were affected or acknowledged in the lives of those close to the Earl of Markholme and his countess. Charles was posted to Belgium. Hendley, having sold his commission, took up his duties as agent and quickly fulfilled Matthew's expectations. Richard and Emily were to be married in the parish church nearly a year to the day after Sarah and Matthew had taken their vows there. Meanwhile, Hendley was a guest at the Hall. With her own accommodations in each household, Aunt Bess would divide her time between her two nieces.

The earl and Countess of Markholme, however, did not enjoy the same contentment and sense of direction as those immediately around them.

True, Matthew thought, they were in better accord with each other, but they had not discussed her charge that he had broken his word to her. That challenge to his integrity still irritated him. So, she assumed he engaged in an ongoing affair with Annalisa, did she? Even worse, she seemed more concerned that "the whole of England" knew of it than that such an affair might exist at all. What was *that* supposed to tell him of his wife's feelings for him?

So much for hoping she might come to love and cherish him for himself. Yes, she found him physically attractive—her eager responses and cries of ecstasy were genuine. But did she understand, let alone value, the qualities of character that made him who and what he was as a person?

The current situation was not perfect, but why risk what they did have on a mere possibility of improving it? Why make himself emotionally vulnerable? He had made that mistake once. Best withhold any final commitment of self until he was sure of her feelings for him.

Sarah condemned her cowardice in not confronting Matthew about Annalisa. She might learn more than she wanted to know. If she asked him directly, he would probably tell her the truth about him and the blond beauty. But could she bear that truth?

She had not yet informed him of his impending fatherhood. In the end, she did not have to tell him outright. She was lying contentedly at his side one night as he caressed her body idly with one hand, her head cradled by his other arm. His hand stilled over her belly.

"Sarah?"

"Mmm?" she murmured sleepily.

"Have you put on weight?"

Instantly, she was fully awake and wary. She did not answer him immediately.

"Sarah?"

She pushed his hand aside and turned toward him. He had not yet put out the bedside lamp. "Would you object to a plump wife?" she asked evasively.

"Probably not. Am I going to have one?"

"For a while." She watched his face as this response registered.

"Sarah! Are you . . . are we . . . ?" Delight and concern warred in his expression.

"Yes," she said softly. "We are going to have a babe."

"Wonderful." His voice held a measure of awe. A moment later, there was also a measure of pain as he asked, "Why have you not told me?"

"I—I was afraid," she whispered.

"Why? Surely, you knew I would be happy about it?"

"I was afraid you would not want to . . . you might not want me . . ."

"Not want you?"

"I mean . . . well, we have gotten the heir. Our contract is fulfilled."

Embarrassed and confused, she gently twisted a strand of hair on his chest. She looked at him and quickly averted her eyes from his solemn stare.

"Our contract?" he echoed.

"You said once we got the heir, we would both be free to go our separate ways." She tried to stifle the sad regret in her tone.

"Goose." He chuckled softly into her hair. "You cannot honestly think I could quit wanting you because we had met a contract." He pulled back slightly to look into her eyes. "Besides, I do not care for a contract that calls for our going separate ways. Do you?"

"No. But you said . . ."

"Never mind the contract—and those wills, Sarah. This is just you and me."

"But, Matthew . . ."

He put a knuckle under her chin and gave her an exquisitely gentle kiss. "I shall never not want you, my love." His voice was solemn, his words almost a vow. He put his cheek against hers and spoke softly in her ear. "What if we have a girl? We would then have to start over, eh?" There was a hint of laughter in his voice.

"You would not mind if it is a girl?" She hated the anxiety she heard in her question.

"No. Why should I? I find this business of getting an heir quite enjoyable. We would just have to practice some more, my dear." This time the laughter was unmistakable as he pulled her closer.

Well, she thought, it was not a declaration of love, but he had said he would always want her. Perhaps that—along with shared interests and mutual respect—would be enough. Many a marriage worked well on much less. She surrendered to the joy of more practicing.

A few days later, Sarah was consulting with Sinclair at the site of the pottery. Inclement weather had slowed construction lately, but the huge kilns were near completion. Both Sarah and Sinclair were vastly pleased with their achievement.

She was preparing to return to Markholme Hall when a young boy came racing into the temporary office.

"I bin sent to say his lordship wants you at the brewery, my lady," the boy informed her breathlessly.

"Was there anything more to the message?" she asked.

"No, ma'am. The gent just said I was to give you this message. Giv' me a penny, he did."

"And it was Lord Markholme who sent you?"

"I—I ain't never seed the earl b'fore. Me fam'ly jus' been ta Axton a fortnight. But he were a gentry cove."

"Thank you. You'd best be getting home before the weather turns bad," Sarah said to the boy. "Strange," she mused to Sinclair. "I was sure my husband intended to spend this afternoon with Howard and the Squire—something about new plowing techniques. They must have finished early."

"Would you like me to find out what this is about?" Sinclair asked. "The boy may have the message wrong. Who knows what a lad like that means by 'a gentry cove'?"

"Thank you, Mr. Sinclair, but it is not really out of my way to stop there on my way home—and it would be out of your way. I have the gig. It will not take long." She left, hoping to beat the threatening weather.

She was not surprised to see little activity at the brewery. It was, after all, late in the afternoon, and darkness arrived early in December. She headed straight for the light coming from the room designated as office space for the brewery.

"Matthew?" she called, opening the door. There was no

answer and the room seemed deserted. "Matthew?" she called louder as she stepped farther into the room.

"Well, now, he ain't exactly here," a voice behind her said as the door crashed shut.

She turned to behold a man dressed in articles of clothing that might once have belonged to a "gentry cove" but were now soiled and wrinkled. He had a heavy growth of beard and his eyes seemed wild with some terrifying emotion. The smell of liquor, stale and strong, emanated from him.

"Mr. Ainsley! What are you doing here? You are not welcome on Markholme property. And where is Lord Markholme? Where is MacGowan?" Fear snaked through her, but she tried to keep her voice firm with authority.

"His high and mighty lordship ain't here—ain't been here. MacGowan must be the feller sleepin' off a hard knock on his head behind that shed yonder," he said with a sneer.

"You hit Mr. MacGowan?" Her outrage overriding her fear, she started for the door.

"Oh, no, ya don't!" He grabbed her arm and pulled her away from the door. "I got this planned. I figger you got the earl to get rid of me. So you can both pay for that little deed."

"Get your hands off me," she screamed, jerking away from him and starting for the door again.

He had obviously been drinking, but he moved fast enough to block her exit. He grinned with no mirth. "Well, now, my lady," he said, her title coming as a sneer, "if'n I had the time, I might enjoy havin' my hands on a piece like you."

"Stay away from me," she hissed, trying again to reach the door. Again he was too quick for her.

"I done told you, I got this planned," he growled. "Now get away from that bloody door."

He grabbed her again and slung her toward the center of the room. She stumbled, but maintained her balance. She was near a big oak table that served as a desk. A heavy metal paperweight caught her eye. She snatched it up and threw it at him.

The paperweight glanced against the side of his head, causing only a momentary pause.

"Bitch!" he snarled. "Now you'll really pay."

He lunged toward her. She grabbed a piece of copper tubing from the table and struck wildly. She hit him once before he jerked it out of her hand.

"I told ya . . ."

He slammed his fist into her jaw. As she fell, her head cracked against the edge of the table.

Hitting the floor, she instinctively curled her body to protect her unborn child.

Darkness engulfed her.

# Twenty-six

Having left Howard at the village inn where they had joined the Squire for a pint after finishing their business, Matthew now made his way home. He rode slowly, mulling over ideas the other men had tossed at him, trying to organize questions for their next meeting. Suddenly, his thoughts were interrupted by the sound of a traveler coming toward him. He recognized Sinclair in a gig.

"My lord," Sinclair shouted to him, urging his animal to a faster pace, then drawing up next to Matthew.

"Sinclair."

"My lord, I never thought to see you. Her ladyship received a message to meet you at the brewery."

"At the brewery?" Matthew said dumbly. "Why? . . . Who?"

"A young lad brought a message. Said you wanted her to meet you at the brewery."

"It was a mistake . . . or a hoax. Who would do such a thing?" Then, immediately the extraordinary insight that had often served Matthew well on the battlefield clicked in. "Ainsley. Compson said he'd been around again."

"Trouble, then?"

"I fear so." Matthew tried to quell his anxiety, but something was terribly wrong. "Mr. Sinclair, I would be obliged if you would ride on to the inn and inform Howard and Compson. It may be nothing, but have them bring some men out to the brewery."

"Right away, my lord." Sinclair cracked his whip over his horse's head and sped away, even as Matthew urged his mount to a gallop.

It might not be Ainsley, but Matthew worried about Sarah's receiving a patently false message. Something caught his attention and he looked up to see a glow in the sky in the direction of the brewery.

"Oh, my God! Fire!" He urged the mount to an even faster pace and moments later, the lathered horse halted in the brewery yard. He could see flames coming from the office.

"Sarah!" he shouted, jumping from the still-moving animal. "Sarah!"

He saw movement off to his right and whirled in that direction, hoping to see the contours of his wife. No. It was MacGowan, staggering and holding the side of his head.

"MacGowan! Have you seen my wife?"

"No, my lord. Oh, my God!" MacGowan had just become aware of the flames coming from the building.

"She has to be in there. Try to get some help," Matthew shouted at MacGowan, but wondered fleetingly if the man were capable of doing anything in his condition.

He ran to the office door which opened easily enough, but as he pushed inward, flame and smoke assailed him. He crouched lower and drew a handkerchief from a pocket to cover his nose. The heat was oppressive and the smoke stung his eyes so that he could barely make out shapes before him. He moved along the wall, but could see and feel nothing.

He fell to his hands and knees. Crawling, feeling his way to the center of the room, he finally touched what felt like a shoe. He ran his hand up the shoe and knew he had hold of a female leg. He rose to his knees, gathered his wife in his arms, and stood erect.

Flames licked at the papers on the desk. The fire created its own wind to fan the flames and the open door further encouraged them. Smoke burning his eyes reduced his vision to a blur. He turned to where he instinctively knew the door to be and rushed toward it, hugging his precious cargo to his chest.

Please, God. Please, God. The steady staccato beat in his head as they gained the outdoors and fresh air. He sank slowly to his knees and gently laid Sarah on the ground. He was momentarily overcome by a fit of coughing himself before he was able to see to her.

Putting his head to her chest, he was overjoyed to find a heartbeat. His arm and hand felt sticky where he had cradled her head. Blood. How badly was she hurt? As he examined the wound, he became vaguely aware of a maelstrom of activity around him.

Sinclair had returned along with Howard and Compson and fully half the village. A few minutes later, MacGowan arrived with men who had gone home a short time before. This small army began fighting the flames.

Matthew's mind registered little of this activity. His concern was Sarah. He called her name over and over, trying to elicit a response from her. Please, God, let her be all right.

She was breathing and the blood seemed to have stopped flowing, but he could feel a large bump on the side of her head. He felt along her arms and legs to determine that she had no broken bones. He picked her up and started toward his horse, knowing he could get her home quicker on his mount than in her gig. He ordered someone to go for a doctor.

Hours later, an exhausted Matthew still sat by his wife's bed. The doctor had come and gone.

"Will she be all right?" Matthew had asked, worriedly.

"I think so, my lord. She has a concussion. No telling how long she will be unconscious. The longer she is, the more worrisome it will be. On the other hand, the longer she is unaware, the less pain she suffers. I would expect her to be oblivious to us for a few hours yet."

"But she will be all right?"

"I believe so. She suffered a severe blow, but aside from the knot on her head and the bruise on her jaw, she seems fine. Also, she seems in no immediate danger of losing the babe."

"Are you sure?"

"As sure as I can be under the circumstances."

The doctor gave him some powders for pain when she awoke and promised to return in the morning.

The house had been eerily quiet ever since Matthew had climbed the stairs with the limp form of his wife. He had called Betsy in to watch over her as he had gone for a bath and to have his burned hands bandaged. Now he was back, watching anxiously the rise and fall of her chest as she breathed. He was instantly alert when she occasionally emitted a soft groan.

Why had he not told her he loved her? It seemed to him he had always loved her. Ridiculous, he chided himself. You only met her a year ago. Yet somehow this past year had been fuller, richer than any before it. She has become my anchor, my hope, my partner, my friend. I cannot lose her.

About two hours after he took up his vigil, Sarah began to move about and moan audibly. She uttered incoherent words. Then she lay still and her eyes opened. She looked directly at him but seemed not to see him.

"Where is Matthew?" These words were clear and distinct.

"I am right here, my darling." He moved from the chair to kneel by the bed. He put his arm on the pillow above her head, careful of her wound, and held her hand with his other hand. He leaned in close to her ear. "I am here, my love. I will not leave you."

"I want Matthew."

"Sshh. I am here, Sarah. You are all right, sweetheart." He smoothed her hair back tenderly and stroked her cheek, murmuring comforting words to her. Her fingers curled around his and she seemed to relax.

He must have dozed still kneeling at her side, his head next to hers on the pillow, her hand still gripping his. When he awoke, both legs were stiff and the one that had been injured ached painfully. A faint light seeped around the window coverings. Dawn.

He gently disengaged his hand from hers and tried to rise. He made it on the second try and crossed to the window to open the drapes. He walked around the room to limber up his legs.

"Matthew?" she called.

Instantly, he was at her side again. She was awake and this time seemed fully cognizant of her surroundings. "Yes, my darling. Thank God you have awakened."

"What happened? Why am I in bed so early in the evening?"

"It is early in the morning, my dear. Do you not remember getting a hard blow to the head? Or the fire?"

"Fire? Where?" She turned her head toward him and winced. "Ooh. That hurts." She lifted her hand to feel her head. "What happened?" she asked again.

He told her as much as he knew. She remembered nothing after leaving the pottery, though she thought she remembered a youngster and something about a penny. . . .

"My head hurts so much—" she moaned. Then she gripped his hand hard, her eyes full of fear. "Matthew! The babe! Is it all right? Please say the babe is safe."

"Sshh. The doctor says the babe is fine. You must not worry." He released her hand so he could mix the powders the doctor left. "Here, Sarah, drink this. It will ease the pain."

"Don't leave me, Matthew."

"No, of course not, sweetheart."

"Lie here beside me and hold me, please," she said plaintively.

He lay next to her and gently took her in his arms. Sometime after noon, they both awoke. Matthew rose and kissed her tenderly, grateful for the miracle of just having her near. He insisted she stay in bed for the rest of the day.

\* \* \*

Matthew would have had her stay in bed another day, but Sarah was having none of that. With his wife recovering, Matthew turned his attention to assessing damage. MacGowan was angry and embarrassed that he had been caught out so.

"He walked right up to me, but damned if I seed the club he was a carryin'! I just blacked out. I am that sorry, my lord. This never coulda happened if I'd kept me wits about me."

"Now, MacGowan," Matthew admonished. "No one thought the man would go as far as to attack someone."

"Still, I am that sorry about her ladyship. Such a sweet little thing she is. Maggie was proper upset when I told her about it."

"Lady Markholme is going to be fine," Matthew assured him. "She will probably be out on her regular visits next week. Though she certainly will not be going alone as long as that scoundrel is at large. Tell me about the damage at the brewery."

MacGowan was all business now. He informed Matthew that, luckily, the damage was minimal. They had probably suffered a setback of no more than three or four weeks.

A day or so later, following a thorough search, Ainsley was caught in an abandoned farm cottage in the next parish. Given the circumstances and magnitude of his crime, he would be transported. The entire county seemed to heave a sigh of relief to have the matter settled.

The atmosphere in Markholme Hall seemed more settled, too. Matthew and Sarah had regained the closeness they had shared in the early weeks of their marriage. It was time, he thought with some trepidation, to face the obstacles that had disturbed them since then.

They sat comfortably one evening on a settee before the fire in his chamber, occasionally sipping from glasses of wine on a table before them.

"I think we should renegotiate the terms of our contract," he said abruptly.

"What do you mean? Why? I thought you said to forget about it." Was that panic in her voice?

"And I meant it. We should forget that my uncle and your grandfather tried to manipulate us like puppets."

"I don't understand."

"I am not saying this very well." He ran his hand through his hair. "I want us to forget about the wills and concentrate on *our* contract—the one you and I entered into when we made those vows before God in the parish church."

She smiled brilliantly. "Matthew, I think you have just said it very well."

"You agree then?"

She leaned toward him, but he raised his hand. "Wait. There is much that you need to know."

She shifted back, clearly apprehensive. "Please, Matthew, you don't have to tell me anything."

"Yes," he said firmly. "I do." He told her of his youth, of worshipping the uncle who had treated him like a son and watching that uncle slide into a personal hell—from which he finally escaped by suicide—and all because he was betrayed by a woman.

"My mother," she said softly.

"Yes."

"I am so sorry, Matthew."

"She was not to blame for his ruin. I know that now. His problems came from his own character, not hers, no matter how badly she may have treated him."

"She was very much in love with my father."

"I am sure she was. And that would have made her a terrible wife for Uncle Matt." He paused and looked into her eyes. "Now—about Annalisa—"

"No. Matthew, please. You needn't tell me. I don't want to know." She turned her head and put her hands over her ears. It was definitely panic he heard now.

He took her hands gently in his own and forced her to

look at him. "Yes. I *do* need to tell you and you need to hear." He told her then of a young soldier betrayed by the woman he loved. He told her of finally coming to realize the full extent of his own misunderstanding of that woman's character and how it had tainted his perceptions of other women.

He assured her that he had not pursued Annalisa since her marriage to Poindexter. Indeed, he had had not the slightest interest in doing so since his own marriage.

"But you believed I was involved with her cousin," Sarah accused, pain and anguish threatening to undo her.

"God help me, I did—at first." His eyes pleaded for understanding. "But I came to realize you were simply incapable of such behavior. You must believe me when I say I knew this long *before* I learned the truth about what happened at the Betsworth ball."

"You learned . . . ? How?"

"Adrian ran into Ridgeley in Paris." He told her the full story up to and including his encounter with the Poindexters in the Meridon library.

"Oh, Matthew. I am so sorry I doubted you. I was just so angry. . . ."

He took her in his arms. "And jealous?" he asked, gently teasing.

"Well . . . yes." She looked sheepish.

"Me, too, sweetheart. Me, too." He pressed his lips to hers in a kiss that signaled new understanding between them.

The next afternoon, Matthew invited Sarah to join him for a drive in his curricle. The weather had improved and though it was cold, the day was clear and faintly sunny. Sarah was glad to be out in the fresh air. As they drove along the lane that extended between the original properties of Rosemont and Markholme, Matthew pulled the horses to a halt.

"Do you remember this spot, wife?" He turned to look at her fondly.

"Very well, my lord. This is where you tried to run me

down with that great warhorse of yours." The twinkle in her eyes belied her words.

"If you had not frightened the poor devil—"

"I should have known you would find some way to put me at fault." Again, the teasing tone softened the words.

"You know," he said, turning to her fully now and slipping his arm around her waist, "this is where I think I fell in love with you—though I did not know it at the time, of course."

She drew in her breath sharply. Wonder and delight shone in her violet eyes as they explored the deep gray of his gaze.

"Matthew . . ." His name was a long sigh on her lips. She raised a hand to caress his cheek. "Oh, Matthew. Do you mean it? You love me?"

"Totally, completely, and absolutely. I love you, Sarah." He gave her a quick kiss and grinned at her. "If you were not already my wife, I would make you an offer here and now."

She snuggled her face against his neck.

"And, once again, I would have no choice but to accept, for I love you, Matthew—totally, completely, and absolutely."

This time, it was not such a quick kiss.

## ABOUT THE AUTHOR

Wilma Counts lives in Nevada. She is currently working on her next Zebra Regency romance, *My Lady Governess*, which will be published in February, 2000. Wilma loves hearing from readers and you may write to her c/o Zebra Books. Please include a self-addressed stamped envelope if you wish a response.